A
FRIGHTFUL
NOEL

The Detectives of Hazel Hill

Prequel - A Christmas Novella

A
FRIGHTFUL
NOEL

The Detectives of Hazel Hill

Prequel - A Christmas Novella

Liz Bradford

Stand on the Rock Publishing

Lizbradfordwrites@gmail.com

Lizbradfordwrites.com

Print ISBN: 9781790971732

Cover Design by Alyssa at Alyssa Carlin Designs

www.alyssacarlindesign.com

Editing by Teresa Crupmton at AuthorSpark, Inc.

authorspark.org

Formatting by Kari Holloway at KH Formatting.

www.kariholloway.com/khformat

Scripture quotations are taken from the *Holy Bible, New Living Translation*, copyright © 1996, 2004, 2007 by Tyndale House Foundation. Used by permission of Tyndale House Publishers, Inc., Carol Stream, Illinois 60188. All rights reserved.

For Ken.
Thanks for being the Doug to my Paige.

CHAPTER ONE

Detective Doug Ramirez parked his Honda Civic in the driveway after a quiet day at the station. He got out and, while whistling "Joy to the World," all but skipped his way to the front of his large house. Paige had promised to decorate their entire house while he was at work, and he couldn't wait to see what she had done with the place.

A snowflake landed on his nose. Unable to contain his joy, he laughed. He and his wife, Paige, had that in common, Christmas was their favorite time of year. This Christmas would be the best Christmas yet.

He abandoned whistling for full-on singing. "Joy to Earth the Savior reigns, let men, their songs employ."

He passed the front window, paused, and tilted his head. It was still dark inside. No Irish candle glowed in the window, no carefully arranged village scene was lit up. *Paige must be waiting for me.*

He shrugged it off, stuck his key in the lock, and turned the handle. He swung the door open.

"Ho, Ho, Ho! Merry Christmas!"

Darkness, save a few lights scattered through the house. But not a single Christmas light lit the banister that led to the second story. No smell of cinnamon. Only a hint of the pine tree they'd put up together weeks ago. No Christmas music played in the background. Where was Christmas?

"Paige?" Every muscle in his body froze. *Think rationally, Doug.* Instinctively, his hand moved to the Glock holstered on his hip. He had been a homicide detective too long. Where was his wife?

He closed the front door and stepped slowly through the entry way towards the back of the house. A faint glow flowed from the family room around the wall of the stairs that towered to his right. His heart palpitated. Was she okay? There had been a catch in her voice when he talked to her on the phone a couple of hours ago, but she had said she was fine.

"Babe?" He always, at the very least, got a hello, if not a hug and kiss when he got home from work.

"Hey." Her voice was flat, emotionless.

He turned into the family room and found Paige sitting on the floor between their ten-foot tree and an open box of Christmas decorations. Air refilled his lungs.

She stared at their stockings in her lap and didn't look up at him. Where was his normally bubbly wife? "Are you okay?"

She shrugged. "Yeah."

If that was true, why hadn't she emptied that box? They had pulled all the boxes out of the basement last night, so she could decorate today. Plus, her nose was red, and it was unlike her to act so melancholy, especially this time of year. But he wasn't going to push her. She'd talk to him if she needed to.

"Is it really 5:30 already? I guess I should get ready." They were headed to the detective squad's Christmas party in just over an hour. She stood, dropped the stockings back into the box, and ran her fingers through her bright red hair. He loved how the fiery color of her hair matched the passion in her heart.

When she passed him, he reached out and gently slipped his fingers around her wrist. He stroked her freckled skin with his thumb.

She just looked at him with sad eyes.

Maybe he *should* press. Something was definitely wrong. "Are you—"

"Doug, I'm fine." Her lips turned up. "Just tired." She turned fully towards him and stepped closer.

His heart jumped. Even after seven years of marriage she still had an incredible effect on him.

She reached up and traced his hairline. "Looks like it's already snowing."

He leaned his head into her hand. "The weather is supposed to be frightful tonight, my dear."

Her nose turned up, even as a smile played

with the corners of her eyes. "But we've got someplace to go."

"Ah, let it snow." He flapped his hand in the air.

"No!"

"But I want a white Christmas." He gave her his best puppy-dog eyes.

"You know a North Carolina snow is NOT going to last a week!"

"Yeah, yeah, yeah." He winked at her.

She laughed and shook her head. She stepped even closer and reached up and kissed his cheek, turned and walked up the stairs.

"You know, we don't have to go," he called up after her. "Especially since you have to work tonight."

"Oh, yes we do. I can't wait to see the look on Jamison's face when he sees his Secret Santa gift."

Doug laughed. Paige had graduated high school with his fellow detective, Adam Jamison, and as if the rivalry between an EMT and a cop wasn't enough, she had gone to Duke for college, while Adam attended UNC. Their rivalry ran deep. When Paige found out that Doug had pulled Jamison's name, she had gone crazy with ideas for insane gifts. Doug wasn't even sure what she had decided on. Good thing she could be trusted.

<hr/>

Selena stopped in the shadow alongside of the empty warehouse and waited for a car to drive down the otherwise empty street. She pulled her over-sized parka around her round belly. The wind was biting, and the looming snow storm released the first of its flurries. Once the car was out of sight, she stepped out into the road towards the highway overpass that towered into the dark sky.

She walked as quickly as her swollen ankles would carry her. No one must see her. Except her brother. *There he is!* Her heart quickened. "Pablo."

He turned from where he sat on the guardrail at the edge of the road that ran under the overpass. "Selena!" He stood and opened his arms.

She fell into them. They had seen each other so little in the last few months.

He pulled her to arm's length. "I've missed you."

She opened her mouth to say the same, but tears stole her words. Good-bye wasn't going to be easy. "I'm leaving Hazel Hill."

"You can't." His words bit at her heart.

She turned and stepped away from him. "I can't have the baby here."

"Then I'm coming with you."

"Pablo, that's a bad idea."

"What choice do we have?" Pablo gripped her shoulder.

Selena looked into her brother's eyes. "They'll never let you leave."

"I'm not going to make you do this on your own, especially at Christmas."

"I'll find good people to help me. I'll give them the baby, and then—"

"You said you didn't want to give it to strangers." Pablo pointed at her belly.

"Then let me go and find someone, that will be easier without a wanted man by my side. Spider'll kill you if you try to leave."

"That's why we run. Don't look back. Get as far away from Hazel Hill as we can get."

She shook her head and paced away from Pablo towards the center of the street. She had managed to stay hidden for the last six months, but that was because she was nothing more than a piece of meat that could be passed around. Pablo was their number one dealer. They would find him. The gang's leader, Miguel Vargas, better known as Spider, demanded loyalty from his gang members. The gang was family, and family was for life.

She only met her brother tonight to tell him goodbye, not for him to decide to go with her. She would run away, give the baby up for adoption, and then she could come home. But she couldn't get Pablo to understand.

"I'm done with the gang life. I'm tired of being Spider's lackey."

"Don't be a fool." Selena pressed her lips

together. "I'll come back in about a month. I can tell it's getting close to time to have the baby, so I won't be gone that long."

"Are you sure they don't know you're pregnant? Do they know who the father is?"

"You'd know if they did."

He shrugged, scrunched up his face, and stuffed his hands in his coat pockets. He walked over toward her and stopped on the double yellow line.

Selena reached out and squeezed Pablo's forearm. "I need you to stay safe, so you're here when I come back."

The deep rumble of a souped-up sports car echoed off the concrete walls of the overpass.

"Here, take this." Pablo pulled a wad of cash out of his coat and stuffed it in hers.

"You stole from them! Pablo, are you crazy? They're gonna kill you!"

Pablo pushed her aside. "HIDE! It's Spider!"

Selena ducked back into the shadows, swung her legs over the guardrail, and hid behind the column that held the road up above her. Her lungs grew tight as she tried to keep from breathing. She couldn't let Spider know she was here. If he got one look at her, he'd kill her and the baby.

CHAPTER TWO

Paige threw her uniform and a pair of long johns into her duffel bag along with her shoes and socks. After the party, Doug would drop her off at the fire station for a twelve-hour overnight shift. She loved being an EMT, but the hours were wicked. And with the storm brewing over the mountains, it could prove to be a challenging night. But first she needed to shake her melancholy. *Jesus, help me. This Christmas isn't turning out how I had hoped, but I know my ways are not yours. Help me be okay with that.*

She gave herself one more glance in the mirror and shoved a loose strand of hair back into the twist on the back of her head. She shrugged the duffel onto her shoulder, slipped her feet into her bright red heels, and headed downstairs.

She walked down the stairs, and Doug let out a loud whistle.

Heat rose in her cheeks. She wouldn't admit it, but she loved the attention, especially when it came from Doug.

"Wow, Paige, you look outstanding!"

She glanced down her slim black cocktail

dress. "Thanks." She walked over to her husband. Her three-inch heels put her at eye level with him. He looked amazing, too. He always looked good in a blazer and tie, but this evening he had put on his best fitted suit and the Christmas tie she had bought him years ago. The black suit jacket matched the darkness of his short hair, which he had taken an extra moment to style. "You're not looking too shabby, yourself."

He slid his hand around her waist and to the small of her back, drew her close, and kissed her deeply.

Her heart lifted off the floor where she had left it after talking to her friend, Nikki, earlier this afternoon. Now was not the time to think about Nikki. She pulled back and wiped her lipstick off his lips. "We should get out of here, Mr. Ramirez."

"Indeed." Doug's eyebrows lifted, and his eyes sparkled. They'd better leave before he kissed her again, or they'd never leave.

They grabbed their coats and walked to the car; fluffy flakes floated down from above. Paige pulled her coat a little tighter around herself. "I can't believe they didn't cancel the party."

Doug opened the passenger door. "We are determined to have a good time, snow or no snow. It's not supposed to get bad until late, anyway."

"Okay." She doubted the wisdom of it all. But this was a bunch of law enforcement detectives. They'd be out in the snow even if the rest of the world had shut down, which in North Carolina, an inch of snow would be enough to bring everything to a halt. It wasn't sticking yet, so maybe it would blow over.

Doug pulled the car out of the driveway, and they rode in silence, save the Christmas music playing quietly over the radio.

"Oh no!"

"What?" Doug turned to look at her.

"I forgot Jamison's gift."

"Seriously? Paige."

"I didn't do it on purpose. Turn around. We have to get it."

Doug jerked the car around causing Paige to grab the handle on the door. So much for Doug's jolly mood. She hated how quickly his mood could change.

He whipped the car back into the driveway and drove up to the house stopping suddenly.

Paige clenched and unclenched her fists several times.

Doug hit his fist against the steering wheel. "Get it quick. We're gonna be late."

She jumped out of the car and scampered to the door. It was impossible to run in three-inch heels. How did Doug's partner, Rebecca, wear heels on the job? She slipped her shoes off as she ran through the house and grabbed the gift. She was back at the car as fast as she could be. "Got it," she said with as much cheeriness as she could muster.

Doug grunted. He had even turned the music

off.

She bit back tears that threatened to make her mascara run.

———— • ————

Selena pressed her back against the pillar, willing herself to become one with the concrete. Her breath shook, and her jaw quivered. Spider stood talking to Pablo near the center yellow line, in the place she had just been standing. The yelling from the other side of the pillar racked her nerves.

"Where's the money, Pablo?" Spider's voice boomed under the overpass.

She fingered the wad of cash in her pocket. If it wouldn't cost her life, she'd take it out to him.

"I don't know what you're talking about." Pablo was an idiot for lying. Spider may be a fool, but he wasn't stupid.

"You had a big deal, and I haven't seen that money, yet. I know you made it, so I expect that money in my hand NOW."

"I'll get it to you."

Selena leaned her head back against the concrete and closed her eyes. Why was her brother such a fool?

"You had better, or you'll pay. You have twenty-four hours. Or I'll find that missing tramp sister of yours." She heard footsteps. Spider must be walking back to his car.

"I'll get your money. But then I want out."

No! Pablo! Her eyes stung as tears flooded them.

"You didn—" Spider had turned back around.

Selena rolled her body the edge of the pillar and peeked around. Her eyes slammed shut. Spider had pulled his gun out.

"You want to try that again, Pablo? Because I don't think you meant what you just said."

"You heard me."

Her brother's words were soft and barely reached her ears.

Spider stepped closer to Pablo and shoved him to the ground. "I'll give you one more chance. Pledge your allegiance to me and me alone, or I swear... I'll put a bullet in your head."

Pablo made it back up to his knees.

Just say it, brother. Stay alive for me.

"I thought you wanted your money. You kill me, you'll never get that money."

"I don't give a crap about the money if one of my dealers has decided to go rogue."

"I won't be your lackey anymore."

"Have it your way." Spider raised the gun to Pablo's head.

Selena turned away and pressed her body against the pillar. *No!* Silent tears cascaded out of her eyes.

Pkew!

CHAPTER THREE

Doug popped a carrot into his mouth and watched his wife laughing with his partner across the squad room. Paige was laughing, but he could still tell something was bothering her. He deserved to be put before a firing squad for the way he acted in the car. It had been a great opportunity for her to talk, she often did in the car, but no, he had to lose his temper over a five-minute delay. They had still arrived at the party before most everyone else, so what was his deal?

"Hey, old man." Adam walked up to Doug in a designer suit, head held high.

"Jamison."

The tall, younger detective smiled at him. "Seven years later, and I still can't believe you married Paige Doyle. I'm surprised she married such an old man."

Doug's mind jettisoned him back to the moment he first spotted Paige standing amidst the crowd at the Christmas tree lighting in downtown Hazel Hill.

Adam elbowed him, jerking him back to the present.

"Jamison, I'm only eight years older than the two of you."

"Still old." Adam tried to keep his voice flat, but Doug didn't miss the quick smile that Adam suppressed.

Doug couldn't suppress his laughter. "Shut up."

Adam laughed. "In all seriousness, you guys look great tonight."

Doug crossed his arms and bit back his laughter. It was a good thing he considered Adam a friend, and Doug knew Adam's intentions were pure. But what did it hurt to dish out a little faux defensiveness? "Lumping me in with your compliment of my wife? I see how it is. Get your eyes off of her. She's mine."

Adam put his hands up. "Whoa. I can appreciate a woman from afar. You know you have nothing to fear from me. Even I have rules about women."

Doug laughed. Jamison was a player, but he was respectful. Paige had dated him briefly in high school, but they hadn't gotten serious. Then again, Adam didn't get serious with anyone.

Adam set his hand on Doug's shoulder. "You should apologize to her."

"For what?"

Adam lifted his hand. "I don't know, but you have that look on your face that you always have after you have a fight with her."

Doug ran a hand down his suit jacket. Being a

detective was great until you realize you work with other detectives, who have an uncanny way of reading situations. He shook his head. "I will."

Someone turned the Christmas music up, and Jamison said, "Guess it's time to dance."

"Did you bring someone tonight?"

"Nah. No one worth bringing right now. But I'll find someone," Adam said. "My cousin's here without her husband, so maybe I'll cheer her up."

Doug spotted Jamison's cousin, Jocelyn, the department's forensic photographer, not too far from where Paige stood.

Doug nodded to Jamison and joined his wife. He was unsure how she'd react to him right now, but he slid his hand around her waist anyway. She leaned into him, and his heart lifted. "Sorry to interrupt, but looks like it's time to dance. Would you do me the honor, Mrs. Ramirez?"

"Of course." Paige turned to Rebecca and said, "Later."

"Have fun, you two!"

Doug led Paige to the area where several desks had been pushed out of the way to make a makeshift dance floor. He gave his wife a twirl and then pulled her close.

Her giggle toyed with his heart.

"I'm sorry about the car."

"Whatever."

"Not whatever. I love you."

"I know." Tears beaded in her eyes, but she quickly blinked them away.

"What's going on?"

"Nothing. Let's just dance." Her lips turned up, but her eyes didn't follow.

Why wouldn't she talk to him? Despite the tempo and upbeat nature of the song, Doug pulled Paige closer. She didn't fight him or push him away. They danced without any more words for another two songs.

"Ramirez, Palmer." The Captain's voice boomed through the squad room.

Dread filled Doug's gut.

Paige lifted her head and looked him in the eye. "Guess I'm not the only one working tonight."

"Would seem not. I'll be back in a minute."

She nodded.

He turned and met Rebecca on the way to the Captain's office. He raised his eyebrows to her.

She shrugged. "Maybe your dancing is so bad that Baker had to think of something." Her eyebrows were raised, and her lips puckered to the side.

"Shut up."

They turned into the Captain's office, and Rebecca said, "What's up, Captain?"

"We've got a body under the I40 overpass at 8th Street. Squad cars are en route. Get there as fast as you can."

Doug swallowed. "Yes, sir."

Rebecca nodded, and they both turned to leave the Captain's office. "That area... heavy gang activity, right?" Rebecca bit her lip.

Doug cracked his knuckles. "Yep." Rebecca was a good partner, but she had only been a detective for a little over a year. They had been partners since she was promoted, but gang cases made him nervous, even when he worked with a seasoned detective.

"You're taking lead on this one, right?" Rebecca asked.

"Yeah."

He saw her shoulders relax a little. He wasn't the only one unsettled by the idea of a gang-related case. Maybe he shouldn't have worn his best suit.

———————— • ————————

Paige massaged the palm of her hand with her thumb. She wished she knew what Doug and Rebecca were getting called out on, then she could worry about that rather than replaying her conversation with Nikki over and over again.

Adam spun Jocelyn around one too many times, sending her stumbling toward Paige. She snickered, reached out, and offered her hand to Jocelyn.

Jocelyn grabbed her hand. "Hey, Paige. You having a good night?" Jocelyn steadied herself and squeezed Paige's hand.

It could be better. "Sure. I'm assuming you talked to Nikki. She called me this afternoon."

"Of course. She told you?" Jocelyn tilted her head to the side.

Paige nodded. She wanted to be happy for their friend, but it was a struggle right now.

Sadness flickered across Jocelyn's face. Was she struggling with the news, too?

Jocelyn's phone buzzed, and she pulled it out of her little purse hanging across her body. "Looks like I'm headed out of here. Guess that shouldn't surprise me if Doug and Rebecca got called out. I'll talk to you later, Paige."

"Bye, Jocelyn." *So much for getting to talk to someone.*

Doug walked back across the room with serious eyes. His jolly expression replaced with his work face.

"I'm sorry, babe, but we've got to work."

Tears cut to her eyes. *What on earth?* "Okay, be careful."

"We will be." He pulled her into a hug and squeezed her tightly.

She had a difficult time letting him go. She just wanted to stay in his arms.

He kissed her cheek and winked at her.

Her cheeks warmed, and she tried to give him a smile.

He looked deep into her eyes. "I love you."

"I know. Go catch your bad guy."

He turned and walked away.

She wished she had talked to him. Why was she avoiding what was bothering her? "Doug, wait." Tears stung her eyes. That's why she was avoiding it. She bit the tears back.

He turned back with eyebrows raised.

She put her palm out. "Keys. I have to get to work too."

He smiled, pulled the keys out of his pocket, and tossed them to her.

"Thanks."

"You stay safe tonight, too."

She nodded.

He and Rebecca disappeared out the door.

"He'll be okay."

She looked up at Adam. "I know."

"I mean it's not like he's headed to find a murdered body with a snow storm brewing outside."

She turned and smacked Adam's arm with the back of her hand. "You are so *not* helpful!"

———— • ————

Selena ran out from behind the pillar for the second time. She had run out as soon as Spider squealed away, but before she could reach Pablo, a blue pickup truck drove by. She had ducked back behind the pillar until the stupid truck had driven away again. Finally, she collapsed next to her brother's lifeless body.

"Pablo..." Tears poured down her face. She wiped his long, bloody hair away from his face. How was she going to do this on her own? She could go off and have the baby if she knew she was coming back to her brother. He was all she had. Now she had no one.

She lay her head on Pablo's chest. Her heart ached as her tears soaked her brother's sweatshirt. He had been the one to raise her after their mom overdosed when she was eight. He had made sure she always went to school and had food on the table at least once a day. He had watched over her the best he could. He hadn't been able to stop Spider nine months ago, but no one stood in Spider's way. He always got what he wanted. If Pablo had been there that night, Spider would probably have died. But now, Pablo could never protect her again.

Selena lifted her head and wiped her nose on her sleeve. She had to get out of there. If Spider's guys came around, she'd be dead. She had to look out for the baby. Some couple out there wanted this baby, even if she didn't. Some couple could give this child the life it deserved, a better life than she had ever had. A life outside of the gang.

Police sirens filled the air.

"I love you, Pablo."

She stood and ran. Just as she reached the pillar where she'd hid, a sharp pain constricted her belly. She couldn't breathe. The squad cars were getting closer. She dove behind the pillar again and tried to steady her breathing, but the grief was seizing her heart as the contraction seized her abdomen.

Three cop cars pulled under the overpass and stopped abruptly. She looked for options to get away without being seen. If the cops found her, so would Spider. She wouldn't be safe with the cops. Spider had ears everywhere, and she suspected that included a dirty cop or two.

To her left a street light stood at the corner. She'd be spotted in an instant. A thick grove of trees stood just past the exit ramp to her right. If she sneaked along the edge of the concrete structure, maybe she'd be able to inch along the outside far enough to be able to run across the ramp and get to the trees. The only problem was the snow was starting to stick, and her footprints would give away her trail, but that was a risk she'd have to take.

Another squad car pulled up with its lights pointed directly to her exit route. There was no way to make it across without being seen. Her only bet now was to wait it out and hope the cops did a pathetic job of sweeping the area. Why was this happening to her?

God, if you're real, I really could use a little help about now.

CHAPTER FOUR

Doug glanced across the department's sedan at Rebecca. As was their usual, she drove. She had insisted on changing before they left, because she had, of course, thought to bring something other than her dark purple cocktail dress and heels to the party, just in case. He wished he had a pair of jeans, boots, and his heavy down coat rather than his wool peacoat. He should have known better. Always be prepared, right? Well, not tonight. He'd be traipsing around the crime scene in his suit and dress shoes, and in the snow, no less. Just one reason he hoped it wouldn't be gang related. Not to mention, he hated gang cases.

"You're going to freeze, Doug." Rebecca raised her eyebrows.

Why did Rebecca always have to be so blunt? "You don't have to rub it in."

"Just thought you liked to be better prepared." The sing-song of her voice matched the glint that shone in her eye from the upcoming streetlight.

He snorted a laugh. "I do. Now, shut up."

She waved her hand toward him. "You'll be

fine. Surely, this will be an open-and-closed case, and you can get home to your exquisite wife."

His heart sank at the mention of Paige. What was going on with her tonight? "If only she'd be home."

"Oh, then we have all night to solve the case."

"Don't you want to get home to Callie?" He knew Rebecca hated working at night and would rather be home with her four-year-old daughter.

"She was already planning on sleeping at my sister's tonight."

"So we do have until morning. Unless of course you want some sleep."

Rebecca laughed. "Sleep? Overrated. How about this? If we solve this case by morning, I'll buy breakfast. If we don't... you buy."

"If it is gang related, neither of us will be eating breakfast."

Rebecca pulled up to the crime scene. Doug got out of the car and buttoned his peacoat. He really wished he had a hat, too. He stuffed his hands in his pockets and matched Rebecca's stride.

"Please tell me this not a gang hit," he said to Gavin Riley, the uniformed officer standing next to the body.

"One point-blank to the forehead—"

Doug's mind flashed back to his cousin's lifeless body.

"—Wallet in his pocket, identifies him as Pablo Torres."

"You've already been here five minutes. What more do you have?"

"Ramirez... I know you don't want this to be gang hit...However, based on the spider tattoo on his neck, I'd venture to say we're...." Gavin's voice trailed off.

Doug closed his eyes, and his lungs deflated. He hated gang cases. He knelt next to the body on dry ground, as the snow had yet to blow its way this far under the overpass. The man was young, practically still a boy. "How old?" His voice cracked.

Gavin looked down at the wallet still in his hand. "Twenty-two next month."

Same age his cousin had been. Doug shook his head, and then he looked at Gavin. "W... Who..."

"Witness?"

Doug nodded. *That's* what he was trying to ask.

"Passerby. Didn't stop, just said they thought they saw a body on the ground under the bridge."

Doug looked at Rebecca. "So, what do you think, Palmer, rival gang hit or something else?" He had a job to do, and part of that was training the younger detective. Plus, he preferred hearing what others were processing about the scene before he gave his two cents. He'd been doing it since taking Rebecca under his wing. But he hated dragging her into the gang world.

"Hmm..." Rebecca twirled a loose strand of

hair. "I don't have enough information yet, but I'd lean towards inside job. This was not a drive by, it was an execution."

"I agree." He stood and looked around. He raised his voice, so the uniformed officers scattered around would hear him. "Let's comb the area on the off chance the weapon was ditched. Look for any signs of someone running off. Go!"

The medical examiner's van pulled up along with the crime-scene techs. After filling them in, he and Rebecca joined the search.

"Ramirez?" Rebecca stepped closer to him.

Doug looked at Rebecca.

"So much for breakfast."

"We might be in for a four day fast." Doug rubbed his hands together. The likelihood of them ever solving a gang-related homicide in the next twelve hours was slim, slimmer than a piece of paper, if they even solved it at all. The gangs in Hazel Hill were just like every other place in the country. Ruthless and tight lipped. No one would turn on the gang member who did this, because if they did, they'd end up just like that guy. Doug stomach churned. He hated gang cases. He hated gangs.

———— • ————

At the firehouse, Paige slid out of her coat and shook off the snow. She flung her duffel bag back on her shoulder and walked into the large common room. Her shift didn't start for another hour, but she wasn't about to hang around the detectives' Christmas party without Doug.

A loud whistle came from across the room.

A group of the guys were sitting on the couches. "Looking good, Paige!"

"Wow! Girl!"

She shook her head and ignored them. She ducked into the kitchen and nearly ran into Caleb Johnson. She asked, "What are you doing here already?"

He smiled. "I could ask you the same. I didn't want to deal with the snow. Aren't you supposed to be out partying right now?"

"Doug got called out, plus I'm tired. I'm going to try to catch a little shut-eye before our shift."

"Get some sleep, then. I'll tell those buffoons to shut it. Doug is the only one allowed to hoot and holler over you. You do look nice, though."

"Thanks. I'm going to put my ear plugs in. Wake me when our shift starts."

He nodded and disappeared into the common room. She was grateful for a wonderful partner like Caleb. He watched out for her, which Doug very much appreciated.

She stuck her lunch bag in the fridge and went to the locker rooms to change. It was fun to dress up, but she was so glad to be out of the tight dress and heels. Even her uniform was more comfortable.

She went into the dorm room, to the back corner, and sat on the edge of the bed. A fresh wave of self-pity washed over her. *No! I can't think like this.*

She lay down, and the tears came regardless of her willing them not to. Christmas was supposed to be a happy time of year, so why was she so depressed? She wiped her face and turned her back to the door. *Jesus...* She didn't know what to pray, maybe she was just tired.

CHAPTER FIVE

Doug was feeling completely unprepared. He didn't even have his flashlight or knife. At least he had his gun and badge, but he never left home without those. He was relying on the light of Rebecca's flashlight as they moved across the other side of the overpass. They were coming up on the pillars that held the interstate firmly above their heads. Up in the recesses, where the ground met the bridge, would be a perfect place to stuff a gun.

The sound of sniffling stopped Doug. He reached out and grabbed Rebecca's arm. She scrunched up her face as she glared at him. He lifted his finger to his mouth and cupped his ear.

There it was again. He drew his gun. They climbed over the guardrail and crept around the pillar. Rebecca shone her flashlight behind the pillar. A raccoon stared back at them with big eyes. It ran up into a crevice under the highway.

Rebecca's shoulders slumped. "A raccoon? I could have sworn that was someone crying."

"Yeah..." He turned and looked down behind the other pillars. He squinted as he craned his neck forward. He couldn't quite see. He reached over and grabbed Rebecca's flashlight.

"Hey! Doug."

He pointed the beam of light straight at a figure crouched behind the next pillar over.

"Oh, my!" Rebecca's mouth hung open; she pulled her gun.

Doug walked toward the figure and pointed his gun while keeping the light fixed on the face hidden beneath the hood of a parka. "Police. Put your hands up."

Trembling, bloody hands lifted into the air. The hood fell back revealing a young Hispanic girl, no more than sixteen years old. Her dark hair was matted around her face, and her eyes were red and puffy. She had been crying, no, sobbing. But why?

Rebecca walked closer to her. "I need you to stand up and tell me your name."

The girl struggled to stand while keeping her hands in the air. Her coat fell open and a round belly poked out. Doug and Rebecca lowered their weapons, but Doug kept his out as Rebecca put hers away.

"I need to check you for weapons. I'm Detective Rebecca Palmer, and this is my partner Detective Doug Ramirez. What's your name?"

The girl nodded, but remained quiet.

"Will I find anything sharp in your pockets?" Rebecca asked.

The girl shook her head.

Rebecca patted her down. "How far along are you?"

The girl didn't answer, but locked eyes with Doug. Her eyes were wide, and pupils dilated. Fear.

He didn't want to ask, but he didn't have a choice. Keeping his eyes locked on her, ready to catch any micro-expression that might present itself he said, "Did you kill that man?"

Her whole face widened as horror swept across it. Nothing micro about her expression.

"No." The word barely made it to his ear.

He tried to smile at her. "I didn't think so. Do you know who he is?"

Her jaw quivered briefly, but as she swallowed resolve filled her face. Her expression grew hard.

Rebecca pulled something from the pocket of the girl's coat. "What's this?" She brandished a huge wad of cash in front of the girl.

The girl's eyes closed again as she fought to keep up her front. "Please don't take that."

"Is it legitimately yours?" Rebecca asked.

The girl sucked in her lips.

Doug stepped closer. "We need you to talk to us, so we can help you."

She shook her head as terror filled her eyes.

He put his hand on her shoulder. "I know. But I promise you, we will do everything in our power to keep you safe, but we can't do that if we don't know anything."

"You can't keep me safe. Just let me leave. I'll

be safer on my own. I just have to get away."

"We can't let you do that."

The girl dropped forward and gripped her belly. She let out a loud moan.

Doug dropped his hand from her. Rebecca put her arm around the girl and eased her to the ground. "Breathe, in and out. That's good. How far along are you?"

Doug knelt with them.

"I don't know. Almost nine months, I think." She counted on her fingers and nodded.

Rebecca stroked the girl's hair. "Have you been having lots of contractions?"

"Not until tonight."

Doug reached out and gripped the girl's hand. "Please tell us your name."

"Selena."

He squeezed her hand. "Thank you, Selena. Why don't we take you to the hospital?"

"Do we have to?" She gripped his hand.

"I may not know much about having babies, but I think it's getting close. It'll be a warmer place to talk, too."

Rebecca helped Selena stand again. "I agree with Doug, warm is a plan."

"Palmer. Ramirez." The ME waved them over.

Doug looked at Rebecca. "Would you find out what he needs?"

Rebecca nodded and left them at the pillar.

"Ramirez." A uniformed officer called from the opposite direction from the ME.

"I'll be there in a minute." He turned back toward Selena. "Let's get you into the warm car before I run around answering a hundred questions. We'll get out of here as soon as possible."

Selena wrapped her coat around her belly and hesitated to step forward, but she went with him to the department sedan anyway. Doug opened the back door for her, and she slid in.

Before he closed the door behind her, the radio crackled. "Detectives have a possible witness. Hispanic female, approximately sixteen years old."

"NO!" Selena screamed and grabbed his arm. She began to shake.

"What is it?"

"They... they just signed my death warrant. They can't say anything on the radio!"

Doug's heart slammed forward against his ribs. "I will keep you safe." *Even if I wasn't able to keep my cousin safe.* "I'm going to get a uniformed officer to come sit with you while I deal with this."

She nodded.

He turned out of the car and shouted, "Keep it off the radio, you morons! Don't you realize this is a gang-related case. Only talk about it over cell phones. No reporting a witness to a gang shooting over the radio. Are you trying to get someone killed?"

He no longer needed that hat. His head was on fire. There was a reason the cartoons imaged someone losing their temper with fire flaming from the top of their heads. *If this girl dies, so help me... God, please help me.*

Spider fumed in his chair at the kitchen table of his apartment and rubbed Pablo's blood off the barrel of his gun. His insides were all twisted up. He hated killing one of his dealers, but what choice did he have? If he'd let Pablo go, anyone else might decide leaving was a possibility. No. He had to retain authority and control over the gang members. He hadn't done the things he had done to let some stupid kid upset the balance.

"Spider!" Jorge ran into the room.

Spider gritted his teeth. "Que?"

"On the radio... a girl... someone saw you shoot Pablo."

Spider slammed his fist on the table. He let out a string of expletives in a combination of Spanish and English.

Jorge stood in the door way, biting his lip.

"Well, don't just stand there. Let's go. Who is it?"

"Didn't say. I just caught part of it."

"Give me your keys, we'll take your SUV and clean this up."

Jorge pulled his keys out of his pocket and handed them to Spider. "Should we get some other guys on it?"

"No. We tell no one."

They went out to the street and jumped into Jorge's large SUV. Spider drove towards the overpass where he had left Pablo's body. They arrived less than ten minutes later. He could have sworn there was no one else around. Who saw what happened? He parked the SUV along the street about a quarter mile from the squad cars. There was an unmarked car parked on the far side of the overpass.

"Boss, looks like someone is in the backseat of the unmarked car."

"Can you tell anything else?"

"Nah."

They kept watching. Acid rose up from his stomach as he caught a glimpse of one of the detectives wandering the scene. Doug Ramirez. This just got more complicated.

CHAPTER SIX

Paige rolled over in bed and pulled out her earplugs. Something outside herself had woken her up. The alarm was going off. She blinked her eyes open. Time to go. Caleb appeared in the doorway.

"We're up."

"On my way."

Her body felt like it needed to sleep for the next two months, but she forced herself to jump up. She pulled her shoes on and glanced at the clock. A quarter past the hour. Caleb hadn't woken her. She wasn't sure if she was grateful for the extra few minutes of sleep or annoyed. She hated being woken up for calls.

She ran to the ambulance and jumped in the passenger's seat. She and Caleb had a rule: if one of them had been asleep the other drove. As soon as she buckled her seatbelt Caleb pulled out of the garage into a winter wonderland. Paige glanced at the clock. 8:15.

"Hey! I only got to sleep for fifteen minutes? No wonder I feel like crap. Why are we going on this call? Our shift doesn't start for another forty-five minutes!"

Caleb gave her a sheepish grin.

"I really needed some sleep."

"Sorry, Paige... Brennan and Jax had only been back from their last call for about five minutes before this one came in."

"So what? It's still their shift."

Caleb swallowed.

He wasn't telling her something. "Why are we on this call, Caleb?"

"They lost their patient on the last call. Jax wasn't handling it well. I figured since we were both already here, we could take this one."

She sunk back in her seat. The rage that had been growing inside her vanished. She knew what it was like to lose a patient. A surge of emotion sprang tears in her eyes. She blinked them back. "Oh. All right."

Caleb reached into the cup holder in front of her and lifted a travel mug out. "Coffee. Just the way you like it."

Her cheeks warmed. "Thank you. Sorry I snapped. I don't know what my deal is today."

"Don't worry about it. Let's focus on getting to this call safely. The roads are getting bad."

Paige looked at the road and bit her lip. You could no longer see the roads. In other parts of the country this probably was nothing, but Hazel Hill, North Carolina had no idea what to do with snow. But as EMTs, their job couldn't stop for a little snow.

"This is more than a little snow," Caleb said.

"Weren't they calling for three inches?"

"At least. At the rate it's coming down right now, I'd say we'll have three inches in the next half hour."

At least she had good boots and a decent jacket to combat the cold. Doug. Her poor husband would be freezing in his suit and dress shoes. Hopefully by now he was safe and warm back at the station.

Doug finally climbed into the sedan; they needed to get Selena away from the crime scene. Regardless of her connection to the deceased, it was weighing on her. He saw the sorrow in her eyes when she had looked out the car window towards the body and saw the ME loading it into the van. He and Rebecca had been called on by what felt like a hundred people and had kept them from leaving the crime scene for the last twenty minutes. He turned up the heat in the car and rubbed his hands in front of the vent. He then turned around to the backseat where Selena sat. "How are you doing?"

Her breathing was slow and focused.

Once her expression returned to normal, he asked, "Another contraction, huh?"

She nodded. "They're coming pretty regularly."

Rebecca slid into the car.

Doug said, "We should get you to the hospital,

then."

"Not to discourage you," Rebecca turned to Selena with a kind smile, "but first babies tend to take their sweet time coming into the world."

"You've had a baby?" Selena's voice exuded innocence.

"Yeah, my daughter's four."

Selena smiled.

"Do you know if you're having a boy or a girl?" Rebecca asked.

Excitement sparked in Doug's heart. He longed for a child. He trusted God's timing, but he would really like it to be sooner rather than later.

Selena shook her head.

A slight pang gripped Doug's heart. Had he really wanted to know? Why? He turned to Rebecca. "Let's get out of here."

"Let's." Rebecca pulled away from the crime scene and out from under the overpass. Giant snowflakes splatted against the windshield.

The car hit the thickening snow and fish-tailed.

Doug gripped the handle on the door. "Careful!"

"What do think I'm doing? Trying to get us killed?"

"I didn't say that."

"You implied it. Now be quiet and let me focus on driving in this stuff."

"Do you want me to drive?"

"No." The car slipped in the snow again. "I just

have to get my bearings."

"Right. How many times have you actually driven in snow?"

"Enough..."

A groan came from the backseat. Doug turned to see Selena. She was breathing through another contraction. "You're doing a great job. Keep breathing."

Selena gave him a weak smile.

What was her story? Why had she been under that bridge? Did she know the victim? Did she know the killer? His gut told him that she didn't do it, despite the blood on her hands. She must know the victim. That would explain the blood. What was her connection, though? Was she part of the gang? She couldn't be completely disconnected. There was no reason, that he could think of, for a pregnant teenage girl to be wandering that neighborhood on a cold, snowy evening. He had so many questions for her, but they needed to wait.

Rebecca made a left turn. The car skidded across the intersection. "Sorry."

The snow was coming down harder and faster, covering the road quickly. The wind had picked up too and blew the snow across the road.

She slowed the car. "I'm not sure this is the way to go."

"Probably not the best. If it's drifting here, when we pass the farm up ahead it'll be even worse."

They headed up a hill. "I'm not sure we'll even make it up the hill." The car slid backwards as the wheels spun.

"This isn't going to work."

"Maybe I should go down River Road. You think it'll be better?"

"Good chance. It's a lot less hilly. Plus, more trees cover the road, so maybe there'll be less drifting."

"Okay."

She turned the car around. Once they were back on the road, they had been on a few minutes earlier, the headlights of a large vehicle shone brightly in the rearview mirror. Rebecca grunted as she adjusted the mirror.

Doug twisted in his seat. The vehicle was gaining on them. "Careful. He's coming up fast."

"Only a few more miles."

The vehicle stayed far back enough for Doug to right himself in his seat. But as soon as Rebecca turned onto River Road, he rotated again.

The vehicle turned, too. He could now tell it was an SUV.

"Seriously?" Rebecca muttered. "Do you think we need to be worried?"

"I don't know, just drive carefully."

Doug watched Rebecca's knuckles turn white as her hands grew tighter around the steering wheel. Glancing back again, Doug caught sight of Selena's face. She was scared.

"We'll be all right." He wished he was as confident as he sounded.

"Doug..." Rebecca's voice trailed off.

The SUV came up fast, right to the bumper of their car.

Doug stared it down. He wanted to see a face, but all the windows were tinted even the windshield. The passenger's side window lowered as it pushed its way next to them. "GUN! Selena, down!"

He reached back and pushed her down to the floor. Rebecca accelerated, and inertia pressed Doug's body against the seat. He drew his weapon and aimed it across the back of Rebecca's seat and out the back, side window.

The glass of the back window shattered.

Selena screamed.

Doug fired back. He kept shooting but wasn't sure if he hit anything. He glanced down at Selena. She was tucked tightly against the floorboard. He aimed again, but the SUV rammed into them before he could fire.

Rebecca tried to keep the car on the road, but the other vehicle smashed into them again. "Hold on!" she yelled.

The car hit the embankment and bounced up and then slammed back down against the ground. Doug's body came to a jerk of a stop as the seat belt locked him in place.

The SUV skidded to a stop in front of them and opened fire again.

"Down!" Doug grabbed Rebecca and pulled her down into the seat. The windshield shattered above them.

CHAPTER SEVEN

Paige sat on the floor in the middle of the living room of a cozy house. She moved her piece on the game board and smile at the five-year-old boy, who sat across from her. "Your turn, buddy." He had been very nervous when they arrived. His dad had fallen from the top of an eight-foot ladder. The father had a nasty gash on his forehead, but thankfully, no concussion. He had also broken his leg. Caleb was still splinting it, while she played with the man's son to keep him distracted. Sometimes their patients weren't just the injured ones.

The boy took his turn and then shot his hands up into the air. "I won!"

"Great job." She put her hand up for a high five, and he slapped her hand with gusto.

They picked up the game, and she sent him off to put it back on the shelf where it belonged. She walked across the living room. "How's it going?"

Caleb glanced up at her. "Good. Almost ready to go."

The man's wife came up behind her husband

and put her hand on his shoulder. "I wish I could go with you, but I just can't drive in the snow."

The man reached up and squeezed his wife's hand. "It's okay."

The woman bit her lip. "I really wish we could just wait until the morning, when the sun is shining, and the snow is melting."

Paige rubbed her hands together. "I don't blame you; it's getting bad out there." Paige stepped closer to the woman. "You'll be all right to drive him in the morning?"

She nodded.

The husband said, "I agree. My brother's a doctor, so we could probably just go into his office in the morning, if you really don't think it's that bad."

Caleb paused. "Hmm... that could work."

Paige squeezed the woman's arm and leaned close. "I have some lollipops in the bus. Would it be all right if I give one to your son?"

"He would love that. Thank you."

Paige winked at her and ran outside for the lollipop. The snow was coming down in fury. The Christmas lights on the front of the house illuminated the large flakes that fell like a blanket. She jumped up into the bus, where she kept a supply of lollipops for the kids she interacted with. She loved kids. Hopefully one day she'd have her own.

She reached into her stash, and the radio crackled.

"Officer involved shooting. Need backup and medical assistance immediately."

Paige froze. That was Rebecca's voice.

"River Road, just north of Albert."

Doug! She ran back in the house and almost ran into Caleb. "You heard it?"

He nodded. "Let's go."

She held up the lollipop in her hand.

He smiled.

The boy appeared behind his mom.

She forced a smile on her face. "Hey, buddy. I've got to go, but I have something for you." She handed him the lollipop. He snatched it out of her hand, and she couldn't help but give him a half-smile.

After a somber goodbye and one last admonition to get an x-ray as soon as possible, she turned and left.

Paige climbed into the bus. Caleb was messing with the radio, worry lines indenting his forehead.

Her chest grew tight. "What's wrong?"

"I can't get Rebecca back on the radio. No one's heard anything else."

"No..." Paige cupped her hands over her mouth.

"Don't panic. Let's just go."

She nodded frantically.

Spider pulled away from the unmarked squad car. "I'll pull ahead and turn around, then we'll come back and make sure we finish the job."

He looked over at Jorge. He was hunched over. "¿Cuál es tu problema?"

Jorge sat up with a groan. "I've been shot, man."

"I'll take you home in a minute, you big baby."

Spider drove the SUV around a curve in the road. It was covered in snow. He had hoped to turn around in a driveway, but he couldn't find one. He decided to just swing wide, but as he did, the SUV skidded. He couldn't stop it. It didn't stop until it fell into a ditch.

He let expletives fly out of his mouth and slammed his fist on the steering wheel.

"Come on, Jorge, we have a job to finish." Spider jumped out of the car and ran around to the passenger's side. He pulled Jorge out.

"Boss, I can't." Blood soaked through the sleeve of Jorge's coat on his upper arm.

"You will, because I told you to. Let's go!"

They were close to the river, so he walked towards it and along the back of the property of the house that stood between him and his targets, all the while dragging Jorge along with him.

CHAPTER EIGHT

Paige chewed on her lip. Caleb wasn't driving fast enough, but he couldn't go any faster. The snow was making it impossible to go more than ten miles an hour and still stay on the winding roads. They had only been about three miles from Doug and Rebecca when they heard the call, but even though they had been driving for the last ten minutes they still had over a mile to go.

Paige dialed Rebecca's phone number again. She had tried each of their numbers multiple times as they drove, but neither had answered. What if they were dead? What kind of situation were Caleb and Paige driving into?

The radio crackled again, and an officer came across saying they were stuck and unable to provide backup.

"What are we going to do?"

Caleb glanced over at her. "I'm not sure. But we're going to help them the best we can, even if that means driving into the line of fire."

Rebecca's phone went to voicemail again. She tried Doug's once more, but then set her phone in her lap.

"Nothing?"

She pressed the heel of her hands into her eye sockets. Her insides burned. Was Doug okay?

"We're almost there." Caleb turned the bus onto River Road, aptly named, for it wound along, following a little creek for miles that eventually fed the Catawba River.

Her heart raged like the rapids of an angry river. *God, please let Doug be okay. I can't live without him.*

"There!"

She looked up, and in the ditch that ran along the side of the road was an unmarked police sedan. The one that Rebecca and Doug drove. Her heart jumped. She watched for movement, but the snow was falling too thickly through the dark night. She couldn't see anything other than a car.

"I don't see anyone else around. I'll pull up next to—" The bus skidded about one hundred feet from the car.

Paige screamed and gripped the door.

The ambulance turned and slammed into a mailbox that sat along the side of the road before finally skidding to a stop. The bus wobbled as the back wheel hung over the ditch.

"Are you okay?"

She nodded. "You?"

He nodded, and they jumped into action.

She went to the back and grabbed their gear. The ambulance tipped backwards. "No way we're moving the stretcher out the back."

"Hand me a bag. We'll just take what we can to the car and come back if we need more."

She handed Caleb the largest of the two bags that held ninety percent of what they would need; she grabbed the other and a stack of blankets. She jumped down into the snow that was at least four inches deep and still falling. Caleb took the blankets. Fighting the urge to yell Doug's name, she just ran. Her heart stopped beating as she saw the bullet holes on the car.

Doug! Where are you?

A body emerged from the car and brushed glass from his jacket. "Doug!"

"Paige!"

She picked up her pace and dropped the bag from her shoulder once she reached the car. She flung herself into her husband's arms.

His arms enveloped her and squeezed her tightly.

Her breath caught in her throat as she squeezed his neck. "I was so afraid... when I heard Rebecca's voice..."

He rubbed her back. "I'm okay."

Paige pulled out of the hug. She held him at arm's length and picked a few pieces of glass out of his hair. "Are you sure? She said you needed medical assistance."

"Not for us." Doug let go of her and reached for the back door. He opened it revealing a young woman crouched down behind the seat. "Selena, are you all right?"

The girl looked up at Doug and nodded. Her eyes then turned to Paige. Pain distorted Selena's face, and she leaned further forward gripping her abdomen.

The EMT in Paige jumped into gear. She stepped forward and leaned into the car. "Are you injured?"

Selena shook her head but didn't look up.

Doug's hand came to rest on Paige's back, bringing a comforting reassurance that he was indeed safe. "She's in labor."

Paige's heart clenched tight. *But she's so young. How is that fair?* She couldn't think like that. This girl needed her help, and it was her job to provide that help.

Rebecca's voice drew Paige's eyes off Selena to the front seat. "Glad you guys are here." Pain shook Rebecca's voice.

"Rebecca? Are you okay?"

Rebecca didn't reply.

Caleb opened the door opposite of Paige.

She looked up at him. "Check on, Palmer."

Rebecca said, "I'm fine. Worry about Selena."

Rebecca's door opened, and Caleb said, "You're bleeding."

"It's just a flesh wound. I'm fine."

"Don't be so stubborn. You were shot."

Caleb's voice faded as Paige turned her attention to Selena. "Selena, my name is Paige. Do I have your permission to help you?"

Selena nodded and pulled herself up onto the

backseat. The girl's olive cheeks grew red. "Umm..." She looked at her lap. Her jeans were dark with moisture.

"I think your water broke. How far apart are your contractions?"

"Maybe five minutes or so now. They started about an hour ago. They hurt so much."

Paige climbed into the back seat with Selena, and Doug hung in the open door. "I'm sure. But that means your body is doing what it's supposed to for having your baby. Do you have any medical conditions I should be aware of?"

Selena shook her head.

"Your body is young and strong. You can do this."

Selena nodded even though the size of her pupils declared her fear. "They'll come back..."

A chill ran through Paige, and it wasn't because of the draft blowing through the hole where the windshield should be. Whoever shot them was still out there.

———————— • ————————

Doug squeezed his wife's shoulder as they stood behind the car with Rebecca and Caleb. He was glad that she was here, but not at the same time. The shooters could come back at any time, and he couldn't stand the idea of her getting hurt. "Can we go back to the ambulance and try to get out of here?"

Caleb shook his head. "It's stuck. The back

wheels are both hanging off into the ditch. It's no hope."

"Well, we can't stay here." Rebecca rubbed her arm near where the bullet had grazed. Caleb had dressed her wound, and she claimed she was good as new.

Doug cracked his knuckles. "True. It's not safe."

"Plus, it's crazy cold." Rebecca stomped her feet.

Doug laughed. "Guess that southern California blood isn't thick enough for a North Carolina winter."

"Says the Hispanic man."

He stepped toward her. "I'm born and raised in North Carolina. But I bet it snows more in the mountains of Mexico where my grandfather's from than in southern California."

Paige raised her hand in between them. "Enough you two. Selena needs to get to a hospital, but that's not happening, so we need somewhere safe and warm for her to give birth. That baby is coming fast."

Doug asked, "Does anyone know someone who lives in one of these houses?" He looked around as did the others. Most of the houses on River Road were set far back off the road. When they had driven onto the road, a few had Christmas lights peeking out from between the trees, but now none showed any signs of being occupied.

Caleb pointed down the driveway that stood between them and the ambulance. "That one's closest. Should we try it?"

Doug bit his lip and wiped the snow from his face. "I guess so. Palmer, stay here with Paige and Selena. Johnson and I will go check it out."

They all agreed, but as he started to walk away, Paige gripped his hand. He turned towards her. The fear in her eyes shredded his heart. He drew her into his arms. He opened his mouth to tell her it would be okay, but no words came out. He didn't know if it would be. If those guys came back... If the owner of the house was a lunatic...

He simply hugged her and shut his mouth. When he pulled back, he cupped her face in his hands. He drew her lips to his. He gave her a short, but passionate kiss before turning and hiking down the long, snow covered driveway with Caleb.

"This could go one of two ways," Caleb said as they approached the front door. "As I see it, this person will either be helpful or kill us."

"Wow, I'm pretty sure there are a few more options than that." Doug laughed. "Let's hope for helpful."

They took the few steps up to the door. Doug raised his hand and knocked. "Hazel Hill police. We're in need of assistance." They waited and listened. A floorboard creaked behind the door. Doug pulled out his badge and held it up in front of the peep hole in the center of the door. He also kept his other hand on his gun.

A chain bolt unlocked, and then a turn bolt, followed by the handle. The door opened a crack. A gruff voice spoke through the opening. "You really the police?"

"Yes, sir. My badge. I'm Detective Doug Ramirez. This is paramedic Caleb Johnson. Our partners, Paige and Rebecca, are up at the street along with a pregnant girl who's in labor. We need a safe and warm place to be. Both the police sedan and the ambulance are stuck in the snow."

The door flung the rest of the way open. The entry way light and the porch light turned on. Doug squinted at the brightness. But as his eyes adjusted, he took in the sight of a large, burly biker. He was easily six-foot-tall and pushing three hundred pounds with a black and white wiry beard that stretched all the way to his round belly.

"You two left the women at the street with all that gun fire? Fools." He grabbed a coat and a set of keys off the hook by the door. "I'll grab my ATV from the barn. We can get the pregnant woman inside faster that way." The man disappeared into the dark to the back of the house.

Doug looked at Caleb. "How's that gut of yours feeling about this?" Caleb was known for his keen sense of intuition. Doug would go as far as to wonder if the man had prophetic gifting.

Caleb pursed his lips. "Hmm. No nefarious sirens going off, so..." He shrugged.

They stepped down from the porch. An ATV whizzed by throwing snow up behind itself.

Caleb's face scrunched up as he shook his head. "Did I just see a Rudolf nose and antlers on that ATV?"

Doug laughed. "Good. I was wondering if I was hallucinating."

———————— • ————————

As soon as the old man left the barn with an ATV, Spider opened the back door to the barn. He slid his arm under Jorge's and dragged him into the barn. He pulled out his cell phone and turned on the flashlight. There was an open stall to his left, so he put Jorge in there. "Come on, man. Let's get you patched up."

Jorge groaned.

Spider pulled off Jorge's jacket and ripped his shirt. The bullet had gone into the side of his arm. Spider looked for an exit wound. There wasn't one. "Blasted."

"I'm gonna die, aren't I?"

Probably. "No, man. You're fine. Just need to patch you up. I need your help to make sure those cops and witness don't ever speak of this."

Spider did his best to dress Jorge's wound and then headed outside to cover their tracks. They needed to remain in the shadows for now. Doug Ramirez was a thorough detective and would quickly spot their tracks through the snow. Thankfully the snow that continued to fall helped cover the evidence.

CHAPTER NINE

At the sound of an engine approaching, Paige jumped. She was about to push Selena back to the floor of the car when she realized it was coming from the driveway. An ATV appeared through the snow that continued to assault the earth.

"What is it?" Selena's voice shook.

"I think it's help." Paige glance towards Rebecca, who stood at the back of the car, gun drawn. Paige got out of the car.

Becca said, "Paige, get back in."

"You ladies, need assistance?" the man on the ATV asked. His voice was scruffy as if he had smoked entirely too many cigarettes.

"Maybe," Rebecca said. Her gun was raised but not pointed directly at the man.

"The two men that knocked on my door said you did."

Paige reached out and put her arm on Rebecca's. "We need to trust him."

Rebecca lowered her gun but didn't holster it. "Do you have somewhere we could get out of the snow?"

"Of course, y'all are welcome in my home. Let's get the pregnant woman inside." He pulled the ATV closer.

Paige smiled as she caught sight of the red nose and antlers on it. She glanced back down the driveway, Doug and Caleb appeared out of the darkness, and her heart settled a little. She opened the back door of the car. "Help has arrived. Let's get you inside and warmed up."

Selena scooted across the seat, but a contraction stopped her from moving more.

"Breathe through it. You're doing a good job." Paige's stomach felt like a rock. Maybe it was just her fingers turning to icicles that that was frustrating her, but probably not. Nikki's excited voice on the phone echoed in her head. She swallowed.

Selena shifted. Paige offered her a hand and helped her out of the car. Paige grabbed the blanket from the back seat and wrapped it around Selena before ushering her to the ATV.

The burly biker smiled at them and then looked right at Paige. "If you know how to drive this, why don't you take her to the house."

Paige felt her mouth drop open. She had no idea how to drive it. She looked to Caleb.

"I'll drive her," he said.

Paige breathed again.

The old man patted Paige's back. "It's okay. Can I help you carry anything?"

Who was this guy? "Sure." She grabbed the

bags and handed the heavier of the two to the man.

Caleb drove off with Selena; Rebecca walked quickly behind them, gun still drawn.

Paige followed. Hopefully they'd all make it out of tonight safely. She knew Rebecca would want to get back to her little girl. Paige's chest tightened. Even Rebecca had a child, despite being single. How was that fair? Paige loved Doug's partner; more importantly, she trusted Rebecca with Doug's life, but why—*stop, Paige!*

"Here." Doug grabbed the bag off her shoulder.

"Thanks." She tried to smile at him, but she knew it failed. He didn't say anything though, for which she was grateful. They walked up the driveway in silence with the big burly man beside them.

Paige's toes were starting to hurt from the cold. She looked down at Doug's dress shoes. He had to be freezing, but he wasn't complaining. Clearly, he was in work mode.

"I'm Zeke, by the way." The bearded man reached out his hand to Doug.

He shook the man's hand. "Doug, and this is my wife, Paige."

"Ah, your wife? That's great. A cop and a paramedic, eh?" He slapped Doug on the back and laughed. "Well, let's get y'all inside and warmed up. It's cold out here."

Everyone followed him up the steps and into

the house. Zeke swung the door open, and the warm sent of cinnamon and pine filled her senses.

The way her house should smell this time of year.

She stomped the snow off her boots. They all took off their coats.

"Come warm yourselves by the fire. What do y'all need for our laboring friend? Towels? Should I boil water?"

She looked up at him.

He laughed. Her face must be a sight since she hadn't tried to hide her surprise. "I know a few things. Marines are resourceful."

"You were a Marine?" she asked.

"Once a Marine always a Marine. Although, I've been retired for just a *few* years." His smile lifted her spirit.

But it quickly crashed down again as they walked into his living room. The lights and sounds of Christmas overwhelmed her. An eight-foot, fat tree stood in the corner, covered almost entirely in Harley-Davidson ornaments. A Harley-Davidson tree skirt graced the bottom. A little whistle drew her eyes up to the left. A train ran around the room on a track that was mounted to the wall. The mantel was overflowing with garland and holly. Giant poinsettias flanked the fireplace that roared with a fire as hot as the acid creeping up out of her stomach.

This is what her house should look like. She

had completely failed at decorating today and disappointed Doug in the process. She saw it in his eyes when he had walked in this evening. She just hadn't been able to do it. Every time she had started pulling something out she had started crying. This was the worst Christmas ever. Everything was supposed to be different this year, but nothing had changed.

CHAPTER TEN

Doug watched his wife's face change. As soon as he caught sight of all the Christmas decorations, he looked straight at Paige expecting to see her face illuminated with joy, but he had found the opposite. With her lips pursed together and her eyebrows furrowed, she looked angry. Why would she be angry about Christmas decorations? What was going on with her?

His chest tightened. If circumstances were different, he'd pull her into his arms and coax it out of her. But they were both working. He had to stay focused on keeping everyone safe. They knew nothing about this man who had opened his house to them. Zeke seemed like an upstanding citizen, especially since he had served, but that didn't exclude him from being a psychopath. Or was it a sociopath? He laughed to himself. Adam Jamison would correct him if he was wrong.

"Doug?" Rebecca came up to him. "You sure about this?"

"What choice do we have? We just stay vigilant. Let's do a sweep of the house so we know where all exits are."

"Okay. Do you think they'll come back?"

"Living witness. You better believe they will. They didn't check to make sure we were dead, so I'm guessing that means I actually hit one of them. But they'll be back. No way they'll let Selena live, and I'm afraid we're on that list now, too."

"Yeah... I was going to call the Captain, but my phone is dead."

He checked his pockets. "Hmm... don't know where mine is, must have fallen out during all the commotion."

"I'll ask Caleb for his."

"I'll check the house."

Rebecca turned and went over to where Caleb, Paige, and Selena were getting warm by the fire.

Doug turned to Zeke, who came back around the corner with a pile of blankets and pillows. "I would like to check the house, Zeke. Make sure all windows and doors are secure and make myself more aware of our surroundings."

"Absolutely. Make yourselves at home." Zeke walked over to the others.

Doug watched him for a moment before turning to inspect the house. This guy was being too nice. What was his angle? Was this a safe place to be? But the guy had given him permission to check the whole house without blinking an eye. Hopefully there weren't any skeletons to find, literal or otherwise.

In the hallway, he found five doors. He

entered the first door on his left. The small room had one standard size window and was set up as a guest room. A double bed along with two side tables were the only pieces of furniture in the room. The closet was empty other than a few boxes and a wrapping paper container. After leaving the room he poked his head in the living room. "Paige."

She walked over to him.

"That first room is probably a good place for Selena to settle in."

"Thanks, babe."

He went back to the hallway. The next door on the left was a linen closet. Across from that was a clean bathroom.

The final door on the right had a queen size bed. This must be Zeke's master bedroom. Like the first bedroom this room had hardly any decorations or furniture. A large black-and-white picture of a mountain scape hung above the bed. A dresser stood across the room between two windows, both were locked. Doug checked the closet. No visible skeletons.

He went across the hallway to the final room. It was set up as a study. A desk was in the corner next to a window. Across from the desk was a book shelf. Doug looked at Zeke's reading choices. At least a dozen books on motorcycles were on the shelf, along with a slew of classics, and another dozen or so about hunting. Hmm... nothing menacing here.

Doug turned to leave the room and a picture sitting on the desk caught his eye. Four young girls, the clothes and hairstyles gave away that the picture was taken at least twenty years ago. Were those Zeke's daughters? The desire to know this man turned from suspicion to curiosity. Doug smiled as he walked back out to the guest room, where Paige and Caleb were helping Selena get settled onto the bed. He leaned against the wall and watched his wife work. She quietly went about setting out the bag of supplies. A scowl set deep on her face.

"Is Paige okay?" Rebecca's voice came from behind him.

He looked back at her and shrugged.

———————■ ● ■———————

Paige glanced up from the supply bag she had set up on a card table Zeke had supplied and caught Doug's eye. He stepped into the room and squeezed her shoulder, but he kept walking towards the window. She wished he'd stayed next to her, and she wished she could fall into his arms. She bit her lip and refocused on the task at hand. She pulled out the Doppler and ultrasound gel.

Doug stood at the window looking out. A reminder that they weren't actually safe. Would the shooters come back? She looked to the bed. What was it about this pregnant teenage girl had her being shot at?

Paige walked over to Selena and sat on the edge of the double bed. "How are you doing?" she tried to ask in a sweet voice, but it came out flat.

Selena half smiled at her and shrugged.

"Hang in there. You're doing well. Let's check the baby's heart rate while you are between contractions." Paige pulled down the sheet to reveal Selena's round belly. She held up the tube of jelly. "This is going to be a little cold."

Selena nodded.

In less than half a minute the Doppler found its mark. The precious *thump, thump, thump* rang out loud and strong. Paige counted the beats. Perfect. But her heart clenched at the sound, and tears stung her nose.

"Sounds great." She forced a smile on her face. "Have you found out if it's a boy or girl?"

"No."

"Really? I've never understood how people could wait."

Caleb came back in the room. "I talked to the hospital and the fire station. The roads are pretty much impassable now. Looks like we're having this baby here tonight."

Paige looked at Selena but couldn't quite distinguish the look on her face. But Paige could tell Selena was scared. But why? The gunmen? The idea of delivering a baby? She had plenty of reasons.

Another contraction gripped Selena's body. Paige jumped to her knees and moved closer to

Selena. Paige rubbed Selena's arm and pushed her hair back out of her face. "That's it. Breathe."

Paige sat back on her heels as the contraction faded. She wanted to connect more with Selena, so she could help her through the labor, but Paige was struggling.

"Have you thought of any names, boy or girl, for the baby?"

"No."

"No? Why not?" She could hear the irritation in her own voice. What was her problem? Just because she felt that way didn't mean she needed to take it out on the poor girl.

Tears brimmed in Selena's eyes. "It's not for me to decide."

Paige opened her mouth to apologize.

"Paige?"

She shut her mouth and turned to look at Doug, who had walked away from the window.

He nodded towards the door and walked toward it.

She followed without question. They walked into the living room, all the Christmas decorations once again stabbing her in the heart.

"What?" she said without waiting for Doug to turn around.

Rebecca appeared beyond him. "There's cocoa in the kitchen. You two should get some."

Doug turned towards Paige. "That sounds like a great idea." His dark brown eyes were kind.

She nodded and wished she could take back

her biting words.

They passed Zeke on their way into the kitchen. He said, "I put a pot of water on the stove to boil, if y'all need it."

She smiled. "Thanks." She didn't have the heart to tell him they probably wouldn't. He was too sweet.

Doug filled two red-and-white-striped mugs with hot water from a silver carafe and stirred in the cocoa.

Paige leaned against the counter of the small tidy kitchen.

"Paige, what's going on with you?"

She shrugged. She was afraid if she talked, she'd start crying. Now was not the time to start crying.

Doug scooted her mug towards her and stepped closer himself. "You were harsh with Selena in there. I don't know that you meant to be, but that's not you."

She sucked her bottom lip in between her teeth. The tears pushed their way forward. She stirred her hot chocolate and refused to meet Doug's eyes.

"Please talk to me."

She wrapped her hands around the mug. "I talked to Nikki today."

"Okay. What does that have to do with the way you're acting?"

"She and Gavin are... she's pregnant."

Doug took in a sharp breath. "Oh."

She looked up at him. The tears won and overflowed her eyelids.

"Then a pregnant girl... Paige, you know God's got it in His hands. It's just a matter of time. I know we'll be parents one day."

"One day... yeah, when? We've been trying for nearly three years..."

"It takes time."

"Doug, you don't get it."

"I get it more than you think I do." His eyes were moist now, too. "You know how badly I want us to be parents."

"Then why do you act like it's no big deal that we keep trying and nothing happens?"

"We just have to hope. Isn't that what Christmas is all about? Hope."

"I don't have any hope or faith anymore, not in this. I can't. Every month I think 'this is it' and then nothing. What if we can never get pregnant?"

Doug turned to face the counter and leaned his hands on it. He shook his head. "I don't know. We need to pray about it. We used to... why'd we stop?"

She shrugged.

"But maybe it's time to seek some help."

Air filled her lungs. She had been all but asking him to agree to get help about it for more than six months. Maybe she should have just asked instead of being subtle and passive aggressive about it. "I'd like that."

"Okay. Let's get out of tonight alive, and then,

after the new year, talk to the doctor."

"I suppose if it doesn't work out, we could always adopt."

"What about *and* instead of *if?* We could have babies both ways. I'd love to fill that house." He reached out to her and wiped the tears from her cheeks.

She set down her hot cocoa and stepped closer to her husband. Her hands came to rest on his muscular chest, and he wrapped his arms around her. "I just want to be a mom."

"I know. And you will be." He leaned his forehead to meet hers.

"I hope so." She lay her head on his chest and circled her arms around his waist.

"Where's that verse that says, 'I pray that God, the source of hope, will fill you completely with joy and peace because you trust in Him'?"

"Somewhere in Romans. Chapter 15 verse... 13, I think." She finished the passage, "'Then you will overflow with confident hope through the power of the Holy Spirit.'"

As always, Doug had a way of helping her get out of her own head. And he was right. Hope was what Christmas was all about. She had an opportunity to help Selena see that with the Holy Spirit's power, but Paige couldn't help Selena if she was wallowing in her own self-pity. *Jesus, you are hope. Help me to feel it, and more importantly, help me to show your hope.*

CHAPTER ELEVEN

Doug stroked Paige's hair. His chest tight under her head. He could throttle himself. Why had he not realized that this was affecting her so much? He wanted a baby, too, but she was the one with the physical reminder each month that they hadn't conceived.

"Hey, Doug?" Rebecca appeared around the corner. "Oh, sorry."

Paige laughed and stepped out of the hug. She wiped her face. "It's okay. I should get back to Selena."

He ran his hand down Paige's arm and squeezed her hand before she disappeared. His arms felt cold without her. He wished he could kiss away her grief.

He turned to Rebecca. "What's up?"

"We need a plan."

He nodded. "Indeed." He pulled his Glock from its holster, along with the two additional magazines he had holstered on his other hip and set them on the table. He ejected the magazine in the gun. "Looks like I used most of this magazine." He inserted a new magazine and re-holstered everything.

"Okay. I've only got one additional magazine. So, between the two of us we have nearly seventy rounds. Is that going to be enough if we have a shootout with these guys?"

"Probably not. And personally, I'd rather have a rifle in this situation."

"No doubt. But we don't. And backup isn't coming. The Captain called back and said everyone keeps getting stuck. They're trying, but the snow's coming down too fast. We're on our own."

"Well, we could hope that the bad guys are just as stuck as we are."

Rebecca laughed. "If only."

"I know... it's just a matter of time." He leaned forward and rested his hands on the edge of the table. "Maybe we should trade off doing patrols around the house."

"Might be the best bet. And the other one of us should keep an eye out down the driveway."

"You know, Zeke was a Marine and, based on his reading selection, is also a hunter. Wonder if he has some weapons we could borrow."

"Is that a good idea?"

He lifted his palms to the ceiling and shrugged. "Maybe, we really could use a third person on watch."

"I just really don't think we should involve a civilian in this."

"But we already have by intruding in his

house. Sure, I'd prefer to have a few more cops backing us up, but that's not an option. We need him, Palmer."

She huffed. "Fine. You talk to him if we have to. I'll take the first round outside."

"Thirty minutes and back in. Be careful."

She nodded and left the room.

He cracked his knuckles. *Jesus, please help us. Give me wisdom about Zeke. I know nothing about him...*

I should call the Captain and have him look Zeke up. Why hadn't he thought of that sooner?

Doug went to the spare room to borrow Paige's phone. He should go look for his own when it was his turn to patrol. Paige was helping Selena through another contraction. "Caleb."

Caleb turned and walked over to him. "Hey."

"Can I borrow your phone?"

"Of course." Caleb pulled his phone out of his pocket.

"How's she doing?" Doug nodded towards Selena.

"All right. Labor is progressing rather fast, but she's coping well. Whatever happened earlier is weighing heavy on her, though."

"Pretty sure she saw that guy get killed tonight. And I'm guessing she knew him."

"Baby's father?"

"I don't know. She hasn't talked much. Let me know if she says anything to you guys."

"Of course. I have a favor to ask."

"Sure."

"Is there anything you can get Zeke to do? He's hovering close. I've got him gathering towels now, but I'm running out of errands to send him on. He's kind, but Selena needs privacy."

"I'll figure something out. And man, do I wish you had your concealed carry license."

"Next month."

Doug nodded. "Let's hope it isn't a day late and a life short."

"Yeah. We just keep praying heaven's forces into action."

"For sure. I'm going to call the Captain. I'll bring this back shortly." He held up Caleb's cell and turned out of the room. In the hallway he passed Zeke, whose arms were full of towels. "Hey, Zeke, what's your last name?"

"Pollard. Ezekiel Pollard."

"Good to know. Thanks."

Zeke smiled and then took the towels into the guest room.

Doug dialed Captain Baker's phone number and walked to the kitchen.

The Captain answered on the second ring. "Baker."

"Hey, Captain. It's Ramirez."

"Where is your phone? What is it with my detectives not having their own phones in the middle of a crisis?"

Doug cringed. "I'm going to find it when it's my turn to take patrol outside. Palmer and I are taking turns walking the perimeter of the house."

"Good."

"I was wondering if you could run a quick check on our host. Ezekiel Pollard."

"Sure thing. Give me a moment."

Doug leaned back against the counter and grabbed his mug of hot chocolate that was no longer too hot to drink. The warm liquid coated his throat as the chocolate comforted his soul.

"What's your gut's reaction to him?"

"He seems legit. Nothing stood out when I searched the house. Not that I checked every drawer and cabinet, but nothing set off any alarms."

"Has Caleb indicated that he was uncertain about him?"

"Nope. Hasn't said anything other than Zeke being a little too interested in helping with Selena."

"Hmm... we'll let's see. I have results. Looks like your friend Ezekiel is just what he says. Retired from the Marines seventeen years ago after thirty years of service. Honorable discharge. Looks like his wife died ten years ago. They had four daughters. No criminal record. Looks like you guys knocked on the right door."

"It would appear so. Seems too good to be true, though."

"Maybe he's legitimately an angel, and you've got a Christmas miracle on your hands."

"Let's hold off on that declaration until

morning."

"Ha. Good call."

Doug laughed but hoped a Christmas miracle was what they had.

"Jamison and Miller just left in search of a plow or at least a really big truck. They'll get to you... eventually."

"Thanks, Captain. Let's just hope they ain't too late."

"Yeah. Good luck, Ramirez."

He hung up the phone and took another swig of hot chocolate. After setting the mug back on the counter he went to find Zeke. Since the evidence lined up with Doug's perception of the biker, it was time to put him to work.

"Zeke." Doug stuck his head in the guest room.

"Yes, sir."

"I could use your help."

"Sure thing." Zeke looked at Caleb. "Y'all let me know if you need anything else."

Caleb patted the man's arm. "We will."

Zeke followed Doug into the hallway.

"As a Marine, you've had experience with firearms."

"Correct."

"Do you have any in the house? Would you be willing to either loan us any additional firearms you have, or maybe better, stand guard with us?"

"You really think whoever was shooting at y'all will come back?"

"Unfortunately, I'm certain of it."

"All right. I've got a shotgun. What do you want me to do?"

"Would you stand guard at the front door and keep watch down the driveway?"

"That I can do."

Doug followed Zeke down the hallway and into the master bedroom. Zeke pulled a shotgun down from the top shelf of the closet and retrieved a box of ammo from the dresser. "I have an AR as well, but I don't have any ammo right now."

"That's all right. A shotgun is a good home defense weapon. If you'd just sit by the front window and keep an eye out. Just don't shoot Palmer or me as we take sentry posts outside."

"Wouldn't dream of it."

Doug cracked his knuckles. *God, I really hope we can trust this guy. Please keep us all safe. Help Selena deliver her baby easily. And help Adam and Rick get here as soon as possible.*

Paige wandered to the guest room window and peeked out from behind the heavy curtains. It was too dark to see anything. Doug was back out there for his second trip around the house. Her chest burned with anxiety. She hated him being out there. Not only could the killers be lurking, but it was cold and so wet. The snow was at least six inches deep now with no sign of letting up.

Selena whimpered behind Paige.

She turned around and shuffled to the side of the bed. Without saying anything, she gripped Selena's hand.

The girl squeezed Paige's hand. "I can't do this."

"Yes, you can." Paige sat on the bed and faced Selena.

Tears escaped from Selena's clenched eyes. "But what's for me on the other side? My brother's gone. I can never go home. I'm sure they know I saw. They're going to kill me."

"We are not going to let them. You'll have a baby on the other side."

"Paige," Selena looked Paige in the eyes, "I can't take care of a baby. I don't want to... not this baby. I know it's part of me, but it's also part of him..." A shudder ran its course through Selena's body.

Paige's heart seized in her chest. How were these pieces fitting together? What she said didn't fit the narrative Paige had written in her head about this situation. "Selena, who was it that died tonight?"

"Pablo, my brother."

"Oh, Selena!"

Selena sat forward and curled around her belly as a contraction gripped her body. Paige shifted and rubbed the girl's back. Paige glanced at her watch. The contractions were staying steady at about three minutes apart and lasting about one minute each, but they were definitely getting more intense.

She had been able to convince Selena to stand for a little while and sway through the contractions, but the bed seemed to be most comfortable for her at this stage. It wouldn't be too much longer. This baby was coming in this house tonight.

When the contraction eased, Selena looked back up at Paige.

Paige brushed a strand of Selena's hair out of her face. "I'm so sorry about your brother."

Selena gave Paige a weak smile. "I don't know what I'll do without him. He was the only family I had."

"Did you see who killed him?"

Selena's eyes shut, and her lip quivered. "I can't say. He'll kill me."

"So you did? Doug and Rebecca can keep you safe."

The door opened. "You better believe we will." Doug walked into the room. He circled the bed and stood by Paige rubbing his hands together. "If you know what happened, you just need to tell us. Was it someone in the gang? I can see if I can arrange for witness protection. I'll call the Marshals right now."

Paige looked back at Selena. The girl's whole body was shaking. *Who is the baby's father?* She couldn't ask that question right now, could she?

Doug stepped closer. "Please tell us, Selena."

Paige grabbed Doug's hand to stop him from

pushing her. "Your hands are freezing."

"It's cold outside."

Selena laughed.

Paige looked at Selena and rubbed Doug's hand between her own. "That's a beautiful sound." She leaned her shoulder into Selena's.

Selena smiled, but then her face become more solemn. "Can you promise to keep me safe? And the baby, too. They can never know about it."

Doug sat on the end of the bed. "I promise that I will do *everything* in my power to see that you are both safe. You and the baby can both go into Witness Protection—"

"Just me. Not the baby."

"But you said—"

"I don't want the baby."

Paige put her hand on Selena's back. "Who is the baby's father?"

Selena's head dropped.

Paige could read between the lines. "It wasn't consensual, was it?"

Selena shook her head, and her hair fell further into her face. "It's all my fault. Pablo would still be alive if..."

"If what?"

"If I'd had an abortion... But I just couldn't." She looked back up at Paige, and tears flooded Selena's eyes.

Paige wrapped her arms around Selena, but another contraction seized her body. Selena wasn't on top of this one.

"You have to breathe. Focus on my voice. Take a breath in, one, two. Let it out, one, two, three. That's it." Paige talked her through the contraction and as it faded, Selena fell into Paige's arms. Grief consumed the young woman. Paige looked up at Doug. His eyes were moist just like her own. This girl was so young and holding too much weight on her shoulders.

Once her sobs subsided, Selena sat up. "Miguel Vargas."

"Spider?" Doug's voice shook.

Selena looked up at him. "You know him?"

A shadow clouded Doug's eyes. "Yes. Been trying to nail him on hundreds of charges over the last ten years. And let's just say it's personal."

"If you promise to protect me, then I'll testify. The baby will be born tonight, and then I'll be free to stand before him and a judge and tell everyone what a monster he is. My brother's death won't be in vain."

Paige rubbed Selena's back. "You must be the bravest person I know."

"No, I'm not. All I've done is hide."

Doug reached forward and grasped Selena's hand. "Paige is right. You are brave. I'll keep you safe. I'll call my friend who's a Marshal and see what we can do." Doug stood.

The room went black. Selena screamed and jumped into Paige's arms.

"It's okay." Confidence was severely lacking in Doug's voice.

Paige pulled her phone out of her pocket and turned the flashlight on. "Please tell me that's because of the snow."

Doug met her eyes. "I hope so."

Paige's anxiety flared back up, and she couldn't get a decent breath in. "Jesus, help us."

CHAPTER TWELVE

Doug stepped closer to Paige and planted a kiss on her head. "I'll be back."

He left the room and went to the entryway. Zeke opened the front door. Rebecca walked in and shook the snow off.

"What just happened?" Doug asked.

Zeke shut and locked the door. "Would seem we've lost power."

Rebecca laughed. "That much was obvious. I heard a big crack while I was outside. I think the power lines snapped under the snow down the street."

Doug let out a breath. "Good. I was a little afraid someone had cut the power."

"No signs out there of anyone lurking about, but I'll go back out. It's crazy dark out there now. The street lights are out and everything."

Zeke leaned his shotgun up against the wall. "Well, let me find y'all some flashlights and candles. I'm prepared for this situation. Then I'll see what I can do to get the generator in from the barn and get it hooked up."

Doug jerked his head up. "Barn? Palmer, did

you check the barn?" The barn was a good distance from the house, but why hadn't he thought to check inside?

Rebecca shook her head. "I walked around it but didn't notice anything, so I didn't go inside. But it's been snowing pretty hard. If they were hiding in there, why would they wait to attack?"

Doug shrugged. "I don't know. My theory that one is hurt?"

"Maybe." Rebecca twisted her hair.

Doug looked at Zeke. "Either way, Zeke, I'm going with you."

Zeke nodded. "Let's get candles and flashlights first. I have a few lanterns, too."

"Perfect." Doug nodded.

Rebecca reached for the doorknob. "I'll go back out until you guys are ready to head to the barn."

Doug followed Zeke to the study. The older man had pulled out his cell phone to use the flashlight. He pulled a large Rubbermaid container out of the closet. Inside the container were four electric lanterns and half a dozen flashlights, along with an endless supply of batteries, small candles, and matches.

Doug chuckled. "You really are prepared."

"Gotta be in this crazy world."

"Fair enough. Wish I had been more prepared tonight."

They put fresh batteries in each of the lanterns and flashlights. Zeke took a lantern to the kitchen, and Doug took one of the lanterns and two flashlights to the guest room.

Caleb and Paige were helping Selena cope with a contraction. Caleb looked up at Doug.

He lifted the lantern and nodded to Caleb.

"Thanks, Doug."

Doug caught his wife's eye across the bed and winked.

In the glow of her phone on the bed, flashlight pointing to the ceiling, he could see her cheeks redden. He loved that he could still make her blush. He wanted to tell her about checking the barn and his concern about it, but the last thing Selena needed was another thing to worry about. So, he just handed Caleb a pair of flashlights and turned to leave.

"Detective Ramirez?"

At Selena's voice he turned back toward her.

"I have an odd question." Selena bit her dry lip.

Caleb stepped back towards the door, and Doug stepped closer to the bed. "Ask anything. Can't promise I have an answer." He tilted his head to the side and hoped that the compassion that flooded his soul showed on his face.

"I think you'll have an answer for this." She looked at Paige. "It's actually for you, too."

His heart spun in his chest. What could she want to ask the two of them?

"Do you guys have kids?"

Doug watched Paige's face go pale. His own

heart sank a little. "No, we don't. Not yet. One day, though."

One side of Paige's lips lifted ever so slightly.

"Maybe today could be the day." Selena pressed her lips together.

Doug cocked his head to the side.

"Would you two take this baby? Adopt him... or her?"

Doug looked at Paige, her eyes widened with joy. Blood rushed to his face, and tears stung his eyes. "Yes. We absolutely would."

Paige's face grew solemn again, and she shifted to face Selena. "Are you sure?"

Selena nodded.

"We would be honored." Paige pulled Selena into a brief hug.

Selena wiped tears from her face. "I thought you'd want to talk about it."

Doug wiped his face, too. "We've been praying for a little one for years now. All the talking's been done. To God. To each other."

Paige hung her head sheepishly. "To strangers on an elevator." She reached across Selena and squeezed Doug's arm.

"I knew God had someone in mind for this little one." Selena leaned forward around her belly. "Another contraction." Her voice as tight as her stomach must be.

Caleb came back to the edge of the bed and helped talk her through her breathing.

Doug walked around to the other side of the

bed and pulled Paige into his arms. Her body shook with sobs of joy. He held his own tears as captive as he could, but they were breaking free.

He looked at Selena as she lay back against the pillows piled on the bed. This young girl had experienced inexplicable tragedy, but she would bring a miracle into the world tonight. Just for them? *Jesus, is this for real? A baby for us? I don't understand why you would let someone like Selena endure the horrors she has faced, but thank you for allowing Paige and me to have this opportunity. Help keep us all safe tonight.*

———————— • ————————

A baby! Paige couldn't wrap her mind around the reality that Selena's baby would be theirs. Air refused to fill her lungs completely. She pulled back from Doug's hug and wiped her face dry, and she reached up and wiped his away, too.

He smiled at her, leaned forward, and kissed her. Their lips met for just a moment, but long enough for Paige to sense there was fear lurking in Doug's heart. But not about the baby. She pulled away from the kiss and locked with his eyes. "What is it?" The words barely went passed her lips.

His chest inflated with a deep breath, and he pulled her across the room. "Zeke and I are going out to the barn to get his generator. Palmer and I haven't checked the inside of the barn..."

"Do ya think—"

He shrugged and opened his mouth, but no words came out.

"Be careful. I need you."

He nodded and ran his hand into her hair by her ear. "I'm going to call the Marshals first, but we need the generator to get the heat going again."

She nodded, leaned her head into his hand, and covered his hand with her own. "I love you."

He kissed her forehead. "And you know, I love you. I'll see you shortly."

She nodded but didn't want to let go of him. She kept her hand on him until he was out of reach. She reeled her mind in from following him out into the danger that could be waiting for him in the barn and turned her focus to Selena and the baby. *My baby...*

Paige stepped back to the bed and sat on the edge where she had been most of the time since they arrived at the house. "How are you feeling, Selena?"

"I think it's time. My body seemed to want to push with that last one." A mix of determination and fear displayed itself in Selena's furrowed eyebrows and dark eyes.

"Okay. With the next contraction, let's see if the baby is crowning."

"Crowning?"

"If the head is showing."

"Oh, okay."

"You're going to do great." Paige got up on the

bed and moved to the end in front of Selena.

Caleb got up and gathered the things they would need when the baby came. More towels, a special warming blanket from their supplies, a bulb syringe to clear the baby's air passage.

Paige rolled up her sleeves and put on the gloves Caleb handed her. She had only seen one other live delivery while she was in school, and even though Caleb had actually delivered a baby before, she was running this one. She had connected with Selena, and this would be her baby. It only made sense.

Another contraction came on hard.

"I need to push."

"Not yet, Selena. Just breathe through it. Let me check your progress. Baby's head is crowning." The head full of dark hair made Paige's heart skip a beat. "Breathe through this one, and you can push on the next one. That's it." Paige modeled a breathing pattern, and Selena followed.

The contraction eased, and Selena whimpered. "It hurts."

"I can only imagine. But hang in there. Selena, look at me. You've got this. You just need to focus on breathing; focus your energy into pushing when it's time. You'll be fine."

Another contraction quickly seized her body again. Selena screamed.

"You need to not scream; focus on pushing. That's it, push." *Plus, you don't want to alert the bad guys to where you are... so, please don't scream...*

CHAPTER THIRTEEN

Doug clicked the flashlight on and off again and stepped off the front porch. He wished he had his own flashlight, the one he was used to carrying with his weapon. But he was paying for his lack of preparedness tonight. And the flashlight was the least of it. His ears hurt from the cold, but that was nothing compared to his toes. He couldn't wait to sit in front of the fire at home with Paige in his arms... and a baby in hers.

His heart sped up. They would go home with a baby. Unbelievable.

He jumped at the sound of scream coming from the house.

Zeke laughed and put his hand on Doug's shoulder. "She's havin' a baby. A few screams are natural."

"You say that like a man with experience."

Zeke's mustache lifted funny to the side with a smile. "Four daughters of my own and fourteen grandkids. I know a few things about labor and delivery. Almost lost my youngest when she was nineteen and having her first child. Thankfully, Selena seems to be doing much better."

"That must have been scary."

"It was, but everyone is healthy now. What was the phone call you just had?" Zeke kept Doug's pace as they walked toward the barn that sat at least 150 feet away from the back of the house.

"I'll tell you later." Doug had spoken with his acquaintance, who was a U.S. Marshal, and everything was in motion to get Selena into protective custody. Zeke was already privy to more information that he needed to be, so this piece could wait.

"Fair enough."

"When we get to the barn, I want you to wait outside while I go in and check it out. Anything I should know about the layout inside the barn?"

"It's not a very big barn. When you first enter the front door, to the right is my woodworking workshop. There are five stalls, three on the left and two on the right. The last one on the right is empty because that's where I keep my ATV. The center is open. You want me to—"

"Just stay by the front door. I'll get you once I know the barn's clear."

Zeke adjusted his shotgun on his shoulder. "O-key dokey."

They waded through the ever-deepening snow. Doug regretted his shoes with each step. This would teach him. His feet hadn't dried out during Rebecca's last patrol, and they were just getting wetter and colder by the moment. "Seems like the snow is easing up a little. The flakes are smaller."

"That's because it's getting colder."

He didn't appreciate Zeke's observation, but Doug knew it was true. The tips of his ears felt brittle, and the hairs in his nose were beginning to freeze.

As they approached the barn, Doug handed Zeke the lantern he held and pulled his Glock from its holster. He pulled his shoulders back and drew in a deep breath of icy air. The hairs on the back of his neck stood on end. *Oh, Jesus, be with me...*

Zeke opened the barn door, and Doug stepped in. Flashlight in his left hand, gun in the right and propped on top of his left wrist. Wherever the flashlight shone, the gun would point.

The air inside the barn was slightly warmer from the lack of wind. Before taking a step, he sniffed. Freshly carved wood, motor oil, dried meat... he cocked his head to the side. There was something else mingled in that he couldn't identify.

He took a step forward and swept to the right through the workshop first. Tools hung on a peg board. A project Doug couldn't quite identify rested on wooden horses. Nothing seemed out of place.

While the barn was small and neat, it was much too big a place for one person to be sweeping on their own. He needed backup. He should've had Rebecca come out too... but then who would watch the house?

He worked his way slowly across to the front left of the barn. A stall was full of lawn care equipment, riding mower, hedge trimmers, and the like. No criminals hiding. He stepped out of the first stall and made his body flush with the wall. He inched closer to the second stall. His gun and flashlight pointed low. He turned quickly into the doorway and pointed his gun into the second stall.

A body hung from the ceiling. He jumped back. It was just a deer. Apparently, Zeke had been busy already this hunting season. *Doug, you are too jumpy.* He stepped into the stall and searched. Nothing else.

He let out a quick breath through his lips and turned to go back out of the stall. With quiet steps he slowly exited the stall. A shuffle to his left. He stepped back towards the front door and raised his gun in the direction of the sound.

"Put it down, veijo."

The voice sent a shudder through Doug's entire body. "Miguel Vargas." The beam of Doug's flashlight glinted off the gun in Spider's hands.

"You should know better than to call me that name."

"It's the one your mother gave you."

"That wench? Who cares about what she ever said?"

Spider's words constricted Doug's heart like a vice. "She deserves more respect than that."

"Nah. She's dead."

"Did you kill her, too?"

Spider kept his gun pointed on Doug, but lifted his free hand, palm facing Doug. "Now, that's low. She may have been an awful woman, but I wouldn't kill mi madre. Who said I ever killed anyone, anyway? I will kill you, though, if you don't lower that weapon."

"You know I can't do that." Why hadn't he come up with a signal to let Rebecca know he was in trouble? *God, help me come up with a plan.* Doug scanned his peripheral vision.

"That's right, mister goody-two-shoes over there. You're a homicide detective now, correcto?"

"I am." *One without an escape plan.*

"So, now everyone is a murderer." Spider took a step to his right.

Doug countered with a step to his own right. "You *are* a murderer." He wished he had physical proof that Spider killed his cousin.

"You always did see the worst in people."

"I saw your best day. I remember a Miguel who rescued an injured cat from a storm drain."

"That boy was weak and inútil."

"Useless? No. He was good. But that Miguel died right along with Silas."

"Silas was—"

"Don't speak bad of the dead. Especially when you're the one that put a bullet in his head."

"No one ever pinned that on me."

"But I know you did it. You killed my cousin

and you will go down, one way or another." It was time for justice to be served for all the lives Spider and his gang had ruined.

"Take your best shot. You shoot me, I'll shoot you. You know I don't care about killing family. And what's my mother's cousin's son?"

"So, you're admitting you killed Silas? What about Pablo Torres?"

Spider shook his head. "I plead the... what is it... fifth? Whatever witness you think you have in there is lying to you."

"You're under arrest, Miguel."

"You're dead, Doug."

Doug stepped back, but his foot slipped on the wet floor. *Darn, dress shoes.* He kept his gun trained on Spider but glanced down to get his footing. As he looked back up, a flash of light to his right caught his eye. At the edge of the last stall, pointed right at him, was a gun.

CHAPTER FOURTEEN

"Great job, Selena. It's only going to be a few more pushes." Selena had pushed during three contractions, and she and the baby were making great progress.

Caleb wiped Selena's forehead. "We're really proud of you. You are doing one of the hardest things known to mankind, and you are rocking it."

Selena gave him a weak smile.

Pkew. Pkew. Pkew. Shot after shot resounded outside.

Paige's heart stopped. No air would fill her lungs. "Doug." She sat back on her heels at the end of the bed. Was her husband dead?

Caleb touched her shoulder. She jumped. "We'll get to him in a minute. Focus on Selena."

She blinked. When she opened her eyes, she locked gazes with Selena. The fear on her face matched what Paige felt. She leaned forward and reached for Selena's hands.

Selena grasped Paige's hands.

"We've got this. Let's focus on this baby."

Selena nodded.

The door burst open behind them. Rebecca appeared. "I'm going out there."

Paige nodded. "Make sure my husband is okay."

"You better believe it." Rebecca disappeared as fast as she appeared.

Paige turned back to Selena. "Let's have this baby."

"Okay—" Another contraction started.

"Push."

Selena pushed through the contraction.

"Here comes the head! Okay, stop pushing." She checked the baby's neck. The cord! It was around its neck. "Don't push. Caleb!"

He jumped to her side. "You've got it. Just ease the cord around the baby's head. Selena, don't push."

Paige's heart pounded. *Jesus, help this baby.*

CHAPTER FIFTEEN

Doug knew split-second decisions could kill you, but he didn't want to take his gun off Spider, knowing as soon as he did, Spider would shoot him. But if he didn't the other guy would. He stepped back. His darn shoes slipped on the floor again.

Pkew.

The sound of the shot kept Doug from keeping his balance. He fell to the concrete floor. Pain radiated up his spine. A pulse of air smacked Doug's face as a bullet whizzed past his head.

Pkow. A shotgun. Pkow. They guy that had just shot at him collapsed against the floor.

Doug looked back to see Spider turn around to where the shot rang out behind him.

"ZEKE! Take cover!"

Spider fired his gun, but Zeke managed to duck into the last stall to Doug's left. Spider continued to fire.

"Miguel, STOP!"

He didn't.

Doug rolled to the left and then to his knees. Spider turned his gun to Doug and began firing.

Fire ripped through Doug's thigh, and he dove into the stall. He took cover inside and turned to face the entryway. As soon as Spider stopped shooting Doug turned the corner and aimed until his gun found its target. He fired.

Spider fired back.

Another bullet grazed Doug's shoulder, but he kept releasing bullets until Miguel hit the ground. Keeping his gun trained on Spider, Doug stepped forward. His leg stung with each step. He kicked the gun out of Spider's hand.

Spider was dead. The man who had killed his cousin, the very reason he had chosen to be a homicide detective, was dead. The man who had raped an innocent girl... gone. The menacing leader of Hazel Hill's most destructive gang, dead. But that also meant he had killed his second cousin. How had he gone from the boy Doug remembered playing with at their great-grandfather's house as kids to a notorious drug dealer?

Doug cleared the stall across from him and checked the man Zeke shot. Spider's lackey was also dead. The stall he was half lying out of was also clear. Doug then made his way across to Zeke. Doug filled his lungs and steeled himself, unsure of what he would find. Had Zeke paid the ultimate price to save Doug's life?

"Zeke?"

"I'm all right." Zeke's gruff voice held a hint of pain.

Doug walked into the stall. Zeke was lying there holding his arm.

"You're bleeding." Doug picked up the lantern sitting on the floor just inside the back door.

"Eh, so are you."

The front door of the barn crashed open. "Ramirez?"

"In the back. Threat's been neutralized." He stepped back out of the stall.

"I can see that." Rebecca stepped around Spider's body. "Is that—?"

"Yeah."

"So, Selena's safe?"

"Maybe. It's hard to know who else these guys told. But from what Spider said, I don't think they knew who the witness was."

"Thank goodness."

The roar of an engine echoed into the barn.

Doug's pulse accelerated. Adrenaline he didn't realize he had left pumped through his veins. He switched his magazines and, ignoring the pain in his shoulder and leg, ran out the front door right behind Rebecca.

"Hold up, Palmer, we don't know who it is."

She darted behind a tree, and he took cover behind another one. They hopped one tree at a time, covering for each other, ready to fire given a threat.

A large pickup truck with a plow attached to the front pulled up toward the house. Doug and Rebecca kept their guns aimed at the truck as they each kept cover, Doug behind a large bush next to the house and Rebecca behind a large tree about fifteen feet to his right.

The truck pulled to a stop beside the house, and both doors opened.

Doug heart thundered in his ears. He was too close to the house. If they started shooting, a stray bullet could cut through the walls and hurt Selena or Paige.

———— • ————

Paige eased the cord over the baby's head. It had taken a few minutes to get enough slack, but it was finally off. "Okay, Selena, push."

The contraction seized Selena's body, and she beared down.

"That's it, one shoulder out. Yes! You got it!" The baby slid out and into Paige's arms. Caleb handed her a towel, and she rubbed the baby dry.

Caleb came up beside her and suctioned the baby's mouth and nose, and then the baby let out a little war cry. Everyone laughed as joy flooded the room. "Boy or girl?" Caleb asked.

Paige looked at him and then at Selena and smiled. "I didn't look."

Selena lifted her head. "Well, look."

Paige peeked inside the towel. "It's a girl."

Caleb rested his hand on Paige's shoulder. "You have a daughter."

Tears flowed down her face, and she drew the baby close to her chest. She locked eyes with

Selena. "Are you sure you don't want to keep her?"

Selena's eyes pooled with tears. She nodded. "I'm sure. I can't be a mom, but you can. You can give her a much better life. It's always been my plan to give her to a family that needed her as much as she needs them. And you and Detective Ramirez are that family."

The tears continued to stream out of Paige's eyes. She and Doug were parents. Doug. Was he even alive?

Caleb walked towards the window.

Clutching the baby tightly, Paige looked at him. "What is it?"

"Someone else is here. We may need to move you, Selena."

"She can't move yet. She still needs to deliver the placenta."

Caleb nodded. He came back over to the bed but kept himself between the window and Selena.

Another contraction gripped Selena's body. Paige and Caleb both worked to help Selena through the last stages of delivery. Paige kept her little girl cradled snuggly in one arm. She couldn't bear the thought of putting the baby down. It was the only way to keep her from losing it over her worry for Doug.

———————— • ————————

Doug kept his gun trained on the passenger's side door of the truck. A figure in an over-sized parka stepped out with his hands up.

"It's all good. No foes here."

Doug stood and holstered his weapon. Cold oxygen filled his lungs. But moving forward caused a wave of pain to radiate through his arm and thigh.

"Adam!" Rebecca stepped out from behind the tree and ran to Jamison.

Rick Miller walked around from the driver's side of the pickup. It was good to see their fellow detectives. Miller gave Doug a firm handshake. "Ramirez, your bleeding."

"Eh, just a scrape," he laughed. The adrenaline still pulsing through his body kept the pain manageable.

Adam walked over. "That one on your leg looks like more than a scrape."

"We just had a little firefight. I'll be fine. Paige can patch me back up." *If I don't pass out first.*

Adam stooped down and took a closer look at Doug's leg wound. "What happened? We saw an SUV just around the curve from here. Crashed on the road and abandoned. There was blood in the passenger's seat."

Doug rubbed his cold hands together and explained what had gone down in the barn. "Was there any way to tell how many people were in that SUV?"

Rick said, "The driver's and passenger's doors

were open, but both back doors were closed. So good chance there were only two."

"We need to check the area and be sure. And we need to check on Zeke." Doug looked toward the barn just as Zeke walked through the door. His shoulder was crudely patched up, and he held his shotgun like he was ready to go on a hunt.

"There's definitely no one else in the barn," Zeke hollered.

Adam leaned towards Doug. "Who is that?"

"I'm not sure if he's Santa Claus or an angel, but either way he saved my life tonight."

"Then we owe that man a drink. That way we'll know if he's Santa, because I'm pretty sure angels don't drink."

Doug laughed even though the pain was intensifying as the adrenaline wore off. "Let's clear the area and make sure those two goons were alone."

Rebecca put her hand on her hip. "You need to get patched up."

"I will, once we know everyone is safe."

She nodded, and they divided up. Zeke went to the house and kept guard on the front door. Adam and Doug spread right, while Rebecca and Rick went left. They worked their way past the barn and all the way to the river that flowed along the back of Zeke's property. They then worked their way back to the road. The four of them came together at the end of the driveway.

"Nothing nefarious as far as I could see." Rick pointed towards the area he had checked. "I did see some blood in the snow across the neighbor's yard where the guys would have walked to get to the barn. It was obvious that two people had ventured through the snow. Although it looks like they tried to cover their tracks once they got closer to the barn."

Doug let out a breath, and the burning in his chest eased. "Good. How powerful is that truck you brought? Think it could pull the ambulance out of the snow or at least away from the edge of the ditch? We could then dig it out. I'm sure Selena needs to get to the hospital."

"Worth a shot."

Rebecca stepped closer to Doug and put her hand on his shoulder. "I'm going to risk sounding like a—"

Doug put his hand up. "Yeah, yeah, go get patched up. Does the grimace on my face make it that obvious?"

Rebecca leaned her head closer to his. "Yes. Not to mention, I'm pretty sure I heard a baby crying inside."

Doug's heart skipped. "Really?" The pain faded into the background again.

Rebecca nodded.

"Okay. I can't argue with meeting my baby!"

"Your baby?" Adam cocked his head to the side.

The four walked back towards the house, and

Doug explained the situation to Adam and Rick.

Adam slapped Doug on the back. "Well, it's about time you two became parents."

Doug went into the house, and the other three detectives and Zeke went to try to haul the ambulance away from the ditch.

Doug turned down the hallway and lifted his hand to knock on the door, but his breath caught in his chest. What if... Don't. He knocked.

The door opened, and Caleb appeared. "Doug!" Caleb opened the door further.

"May I come in?"

"Totally." Caleb stepped out of the way.

Doug's eyes fell on Paige, who stood about five feet away, a little bundle in her arms. His heart launched into the sky.

"Doug." Her smile took over her tear-streaked face. "You're okay!"

He crossed the space between them and slid his hand under her ear and into her hair. He drew her face to his, her lips to his. He kissed her with all the passion he had. Everyone else in the room seemed to disappear as their lips moved in perfect synchronization like a perfectly performed ballet. The warmth of her kiss drove the chill from his bones.

The baby squawked. Doug pulled back from kissing his wife. Laughter rippled around the room.

Caleb said, "Looks like she's already getting in between mom and dad."

He put his hand on the baby's blanketed head then looked at Paige. "She?"

Paige nodded.

A daughter.

Doug glanced at the bed where Selena was lying back against a huge pile of pillows. Her face downcast. His heart ached for her. He rubbed the baby's head before walking to Selena's side. He grabbed a dining chair that had been brought into the room, pulled it close, and sat. He reached his hand out to her.

She put her hand into his.

"Selena, you have been so brave. Thank you for choosing life. Thank you for choosing us... I have news." He closed his eyes as the weight of what had happened in the barn slammed onto his shoulders. He looked Selena in the eye. "Spider's dead."

"What? He was here?"

Doug nodded.

"You sure he's dead?"

"Yes, along with the other guy that was with him."

From behind him Paige said, "Oh, Doug." She knew the whole story. How he and Miguel were related. How their lives had taken completely different paths. She knew that Miguel had killed Silas in cold blood just to get a higher position in the gang. After going to church with Doug, Silas had wavered in his loyalty to the gang. Paige also knew how Doug blamed himself for Silas's death and how he had done everything in his ability to bring Miguel to justice.

Selena squeezed his hand. "Finally, justice for all the ones he's killed."

Doug nodded and tried to smile, but his heart was so heavy. He had always hoped that it wouldn't come to that. He had prayed that Miguel would turn to Christ.

"Thank you for keeping me safe. And thank you for adopting the baby."

Doug squeezed her hand before letting go. He stood and turned to Paige and the baby.

"You want to hold her?" Paige held out the baby, but then pulled the baby back. "Doug, you're bleeding."

He tried to smile at her and mask the pain that radiated from his wounds. He wasn't about to tell her how badly his fingers and toes hurt, too. "Why do people keep pointing out the obvious? It's rather hard to be in a shootout and not get hit at least once. Good thing gangsters don't know how to aim very well."

"More than once? Doug! Your leg, too?"

Caleb walked over to him and pulled the chair away from the bed. "Sit." He pointed. "I'll patch you up, then you can hold your daughter."

His daughter. Warmth flooded his soul and poured through his body.

Paige kissed the newborn's forehead. She was perfect. A wisp of dark hair sat across her olive-brown skin that perfectly matched Doug's. God truly had picked this little girl for them. Caleb and Adam brought the stretcher into the bedroom. Paige handed Doug the baby, so she could help Selena. The guys were proud to report that they had managed to pull the ambulance away from where it was teetering on the edge of the ditch and clear the driveway enough to get the ambulance closer to the house. Finally, they would be able to transport Selena to the hospital, as well as the baby.

Paige jumped into action. Caleb gathered their supplies, and she gathered all the towels and other linens Zeke had so graciously supplied. She carried them out of the room and found Zeke in the living room, all patched up from his minor gunshot wound across the top of his shoulder. The bullet had only grazed him and had completely missed the bone but had ripped through his bulky arms. "Zeke, where's your washer? I can get this load started for you."

He stood. "I can get it."

"No, let me. Just show me the way. It's the least I can do to repay your hospitality."

She followed him through the kitchen to the little utility closet that held the washer and dryer.

"Thank you," he said. "It's been an honor to see the change in you tonight. You came into my house this evening hiding something. I love watching God change sorrow into joy. Who would have known you'd want those guys dead so badly?" He winked at her.

She giggled, and her already warm cheeks turned up a few more degrees. "Thank you for opening your home. I am so grateful."

"Think nothing of it. Congratulations to you and Doug. One daughter down, three more to catch up with me. Promise me you'll go for four?" Zeke winked at her again.

Paige laughed. "I can't promise that... God's in control."

"Who knew God would work tonight together this way?"

"I guess only He did." Paige poured the detergent in the washer.

Zeke smiled. "Indeed. I'm glad I had the privilege of being used by God tonight. My youngest daughter, Elizabeth, had her baby in an emergency situation, and I've been eternally grateful for those who helped her. It was the least I could do."

Paige squeezed Zeke's arm. "Elizabeth is my mom's name."

"It's a good name. Have you named your daughter yet?"

"Not yet. But we haven't even had a minute to talk about it."

"You'll figure it out." He winked at her and the returned to the living room. "I want to give you something."

She tipped her head to the side and followed Zeke to the Christmas tree. Beside the tree were more than a dozen little bags.

He picked one up and handed it to her. "I didn't know why at the time, but when I was making these little ornaments for my grandkids, I ended up making fifteen, one more than I needed. Now I know why."

Paige opened the bag and pulled out a little red rocking horse. "Oh, Zeke, it's amazing. Thank you."

"May the hope and joy of Jesus fill you and your little family this Christmas."

She wiped the tears away from her eyes. She had no more words, all she could do was nod.

Paige left Zeke in the living room with Rick and Rebecca and joined the others in the bedroom.

Selena was already on the stretcher; Paige squeezed her leg. "We ready to head out?"

Caleb nodded. "Yep. Let's get to the hospital. Rick and Adam will plow the way for us where needed, so we'll follow them."

"Good. We need to get baby some formula. She's rooting like crazy."

Caleb and Adam wheeled the stretcher out. Doug came up beside her, and they walked out together.

Paige reached over and rubbed the baby's head. "We need to name her."

"You have any ideas?" His eyes sparkled as he

cradled their daughter.

"Hope."

"Paige, that's perfect. What about Hope Elizabeth?"

"I love it!"

———————————•———————————

Doug turned the key in the lock. He pushed the door open and held the screen door for Paige. She carried Hope in the baby car seat through the door. It had been over twenty-four hours, and he was just starting to adjust to their new reality. They were parents.

"Welcome home, little girl." Paige looked up at him.

Tears stung Doug's eyes. This house, that was entirely too big for just Doug and Paige, had a new occupant.

They shed their coats and wet shoes and went into the living room. Paige pulled the blanket away from Hope, unbuckled the tiny newborn, and lifted her out of the car seat. Yesterday afternoon, once he had been released from the hospital after his minor frostbite had been treated, he went to the store and got a few essentials: the car seat, diapers and wipes, bottles and formula, and a few outfits. They were a long way from having everything they needed, but it was a good start.

He sat back onto the couch and stretched his arm across the back. Paige scooted back next to him and snuggled Hope against her chest. He wrapped his arm around them.

KNOCK, KNOCK.

Paige looked up at him. "Expecting someone?"

He shook his head and stood. "Nope." He walked back to the front door. He opened it.

Rebecca and Callie stood there, and just behind them, holding a big box, was Adam and Caleb.

"Hey, guys. What are you doing here?"

Rebecca lifted a large white bag. "I do believe I owe you breakfast."

"That you do. Who knew we could solve a gang case in less than twelve hours?"

She laughed.

He stepped back and let them come inside. "What is that?"

Adam smiled. "Thought that baby of yours could use a bed."

Paige stepped into the entry way. "A crib? Oh, guys!"

Caleb said, "We're even gonna put it together for you."

Doug was astounded by his friends' generosity. "Thank you." The words seemed insufficient.

Caleb and Adam put the box down, and they all went into the kitchen. They dug into the French toast, bacon, and fresh fruit that Rebecca brought.

After they had all eaten, Adam disappeared

out the front door.

"Where's he going?" Paige asked.

"There were a few other things in the car." Caleb pointed at Hope. "May I hold her?"

"Only if you promise not to drop her."

Frown lines briefly creased the sides of Caleb's mouth but were quickly replaced with a smile. He didn't know Caleb very well, well enough to trust the man with his wife's safety, but not personally. What about the baby made him sad?

Adam came back inside with the mattress for the crib and the Secret Santa gift Paige had gotten for him. He came to the table where they all still sat and set the bag down in front of Doug and Paige. "Seriously? What is this crap?"

Paige laughed.

"Doug?" Adam put his hand on his hip.

"I honestly have no idea. It was all her." He pointed at his wife.

Paige continued to laugh.

Rebecca stood and pulled the bag towards herself. "Well, what is it?" She pulled out a large, royal blue foam finger that said, "Duke is #1." Then a set of hand towels with Duke's mascot. And finally, she pulled out a mug that was the shape of the Blue Devil himself. Everyone laughed, even Callie, who clearly had no idea why she was laughing.

Adam let out a dramatic shudder. "You can keep all that. Thank you very much." He then walked around and collected everyone's dirty plates. Doug and Rebecca also started helping clean up.

Once in the kitchen, Doug had an idea. "Hey, Rebecca. What about Caleb?"

Her eyebrows scrunched. "What about him?"

"You two could make a good pair."

Adam put his hand on Rebecca's shoulder. "I concur. You two would be a great couple."

"I... I don't know. Sure, he's a great guy, but I'm not in the mood to date right now."

Doug smiled. "That's fine—just a thought."

"One you can keep to yourself."

He put his hands up in surrender. "Sorry."

She laughed.

They took care of the dishes, and Doug went back to the dining room. He went up behind his wife and put his hands on her shoulders. She gripped his hands. He leaned down and kissed her check.

Caleb handed Hope to him. "I'm gonna help Adam put the crib together. Where do y'all want it?"

A smile lit up Paige's face. There's an empty bedroom right next to the master. In there."

"On it."

Caleb and Adam disappeared. Doug looked down at the baby in his arms. He was still dumbstruck at the sight.

Paige stood and stroked Hope's hair. "Looks like we got our Christmas gift a little early."

"That we did. Merry Christmas, Paige."

"Merry Christmas."

He leaned down and planted a kiss on his wife's lips. This was the best Christmas since Christ was born. *Thank you, Jesus.*

EPILOUGE

Doug sat back on the couch, Hope nestled in his arms. Christmas morning had come, and he still couldn't believe that he was sitting at home with a newborn in his arms. The last week had been crazy. With wrapping everything up with the case, his paternity leave had started off a little rough, plus they were not prepared for a baby. The detectives' squad had thrown them a baby shower, even though it was the week before Christmas, but because of everyone's generosity, they had the essentials.

Hope cooed. Doug's heart swelled. She already had him wrapped around her little finger. He offered her the bottle he held in his hand; music played softly in the background. This really was the best Christmas ever. Even though Paige never did get all the decorations up, the tree looked amazing, and she had managed to decorate the mantel over the fireplace.

Hope finished her bottle, so Doug stood and padded to the kitchen. He put the bottle on the counter and wandered to the back door. Last week's snow was mostly melted, as had been anticipated, leaving a muddy, barren land behind, but that was okay. Nothing could dampen his spirit today.

He heard Paige come down the stairs, so he turned. "Merry Christmas."

She smiled and walked to the tree. She set a little gift underneath the tree with the few other things they had for each other. He was grateful that since the beginning of their marriage they had set Christmas morning aside for just them, and now Hope, too. They both had wonderful, loving families, but they were both big and loud. Yesterday they had, as always, spent Christmas Eve with her family, eating a large Irish Christmas dinner and then attended midnight Mass. It had been a late night, so he had taken the early shift with Hope to let Paige sleep.

She walked over to him and Hope. "I can't believe you let me sleep so late."

He smiled. It was already ten o'clock, and they were due at his parents at two. "You needed it."

"I'm not denying that. Hope had me up from three until four. Good thing you're cute, sweet baby." Paige leaned over and kissed Hope's head.

Doug nodded towards the tree. "What was that you just put under the tree?"

Paige's eyebrows rose briefly. "Wouldn't you like to know?"

"Uh, yeah."

She laughed. "In time. Breakfast or presents first?"

"Presents of course!"

"You are just one big kid, aren't you?"

Instead of replying to her question, he stepped closer and kissed her cheek before heading to the tree. He sat in front of the tree like a little boy full of anticipation. But instead of the anticipation of what he would receive, his excitement was entirely encompassed in the gift he had for Paige.

"What are you so excited about?" She sat next to him and took Hope from his arms.

He couldn't wait. He reached for the little square box wrapped with red paper, doting a miniature green bow. "For you my love."

"No way! *You* want me to go first?"

He bit his lip and nodded.

Carefully reaching around Hope, she plucked the bow off and then tore into the paper. She flipped the lid of the box with her thumb and dumped the jewelry box into her hand. "Jewelry? You never give me jewelry."

It was true. Other than her engagement ring he had only once bought jewelry for her. It had been an abysmal failure. The little gold earrings were completely wrong for her. She liked silver and dangling earrings. "I think you'll like this. I've learned about your tastes a little over the years."

She righted the box and hesitated as she lifted the lid. Once her eyes had taken in the simple silver chain with its little rectangular charm her eyes got wide and her mouth fell agape. The charm said "MOM," and had a small stone of turquoise, December's birthstone. "Oh, Doug."

"You're welcome." He took the necklace and clasped it around her neck.

"Well, I guess you have to open this one first then." She reached forward and grabbed the little bag she had brought down with her this morning. "It would seem the best gifts come in small packages." She looked down at Hope. "Just like this little one."

"Absolutely!" He took the gift from Paige.

"This is actually for you and Hope, but she won't understand yet."

He opened the bag and pulled out a wad of tissue paper, under the paper was a three by five picture frame. He grabbed it and pulled it out. Rather than a picture in the frame, a handwritten note was behind the glass with a little, crudely drawn picture of an oven with a loaf of bread showing inside. He read the note out loud, "'We have a bun in the oven!' Wait, what?" He looked at Paige.

Her cheeks were a bright shade of pink. "Hope's going to be a big sister."

"No way."

"Yes, way. We got a double dose of blessing this Christmas!"

Connect with Liz Bradford

Thanks for reading A FRIGHTFUL NOEL!

Let's connect.

- Sign up for my mailing list and get a free short story about Rebecca Palmer:

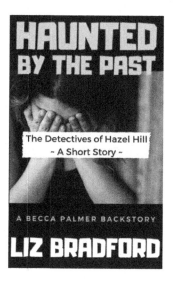

To get the story go to
http://eepurl.com/dGuIjr

- Like and Follow me on Facebook:
www.facebook.com/lizbradfordwrites

- Follow me on Amazon (and don't forget to leave a review of A FRIGHTFUL NOEL):
www.amazon.com/author/lizbradford

- Follow me on BookBub:
www.bookbub.com/profile/liz-bradford

Also by Liz Bradford

The Detectives of Hazel Hill Series

Book One: NOT ALONE
Available now at Amazon:
http://a.co/d/dzIoiSF

When single moms are turning up dead, Police Detective Rebecca Palmer will stop at nothing to bring the killer to justice.

Detective Rebecca Palmer is hunting a serial killer bent on inflicting a warped sense of Biblical judgment. But, with so few clues, she struggles to catch his trail. The killer's obsession with murdering single moms grips Rebecca's heart with profound intensity, since she herself is a single mom. Will she be able to stop him before he takes another mother away from her child?

Jared Johnson fought crime as a detective on the streets of Chicago but has decided to trade the inner city for the simpler life of the south. His brother said Hazel Hill, North Carolina is a great place to live, and Jared is willing to test his brother's claims. But is the move just another stop as Jared runs from his past, or will Hazel Hill be the place his restless soul can finally settle down?

NOT ALONE is a Christian romantic suspense novel that will keep you on the edge of your seat as you cheer for love and justice to prevail.

Book Two: PURSUED
Coming Spring 2019

A stack of missing person cold cases dating back over the last decade... Detective Amelia Banik will solve this case if it's the last thing she does.

Detective Amelia Banik is new to the Hazel Hill police department after not being on the force for six years to stay home with her kids. When she finds a pattern in a stack of cold cases that exactly matches her missing aunt's case, she is compelled to prove herself and find answers for the families. But what good is a pattern if you have no evidence to follow? When another couple that fits the profile of the cold case victims goes missing, she is determined to find out what happened. But will she be too late?

Paramedic Caleb Johnson has taken advantage of his single life to serve the Lord, but he longs for a family. When a beautiful widow rolls into town with her adorable little children, hope ignites in his heart. But the shadow that hangs over Amelia's heart threatens to shut him out forever. Will she stop running from God? Will Caleb be able to help her love again? Or will the case she's working catch up to them?

Book Three: ON YOUR KNEES
Coming Spring 2019

Adam Jamison and Ella Perkin's story

Acknowledgments

Above all, I must thank my Lord and Savior for the hope He gives us at Christmas and each and every day. This is all for you, Jesus.

Thank you to my husband, Ken. Thanks for helping me get out of my head, just like Doug helps Paige do the same. I couldn't do this without your support and patience.

Thank you to my three girls. Thanks for being awesome and such great inspiration.

Thank you to my mom and dad. Thanks for your support and help. And Mom, thanks for always answering my medical questions.

Thank you to my friends, especially Becky, and family who have all rallied behind me with words of encouragement.

Thank you to my editor, Teresa. Thanks for teaching me to use subtext. It is so much fun working with you.

Thank you to my cover designer, Alyssa. Thank you so much for blowing my mind with such a beautiful cover design and with a newborn in your arms no less.

Thank you to my formatter, Kari. Thanks for making my book beautiful and easy to read.

Thank you to my readers. I pray this story inspires you to hope in Jesus as you learn to trust Him.

Author's Note

*I pray that God, the source of hope,
will fill you completely with joy and
peace because you trust in Him.
Then you will overflow with
confident hope through the power of
the Holy Spirit.*

Romans 15:13

Christmas. A time of hope, joy, and peace. Or at least it should be, right? Maybe you aren't feeling those things this Christmas season. Maybe this year has been harder than you anticipated. Maybe anxiety and depression are gripping your heart. Even if things are going great on the outside, sometimes we're still a mess on the inside.

Just like the verse above says, I pray you would be filled with joy and peace. God is the source of our hope. Hope isn't found in the food, the decorations, or even (maybe especially not) in our families. Our hope is found in Christ alone. As we celebrate His birth, let us remember why. Who is this child that was born to bring us hope?

Light of the world - He brings light into the darkest places in our hearts and says, "I see you."

Comforter - He holds our hearts no matter the ache we hold inside

Healer - He can heal our hearts. He can heal our bodies. When we have surrendered our lives to Him, we have the hope of eternity and permanent healing from all that ails us.

Savior - We have no hope of saving ourselves. We can NEVER be good enough. But Jesus came to earth and died for us and declares His own righteousness for us. What does that even mean though? It means that when God looks at us, instead of seeing all the mess, the sins, the bad choices, the regret and shame we walk around with, He sees Jesus' perfection. That is the free gift of God! We can't earn it. It is freely given to us. The only thing we have to do is accept it.

As you celebrate, Christmas this year, whether it's tomorrow or still three hundred days away, let's remember the reason Jesus came to earth. To pay the price for our sins. He came to give us hope. Hope for freedom. Hope for salvation. Hope for eternity.

About the Author

Liz didn't always know she was a writer, but she was. From her earliest days, stories were a natural part of her imagination. In high school, she toyed around with writing, but it was nothing more than a secret hobby. But one day, when her middle daughter was a little over a year old, a story idea crept in her mind and wouldn't leave her alone. So, she started writing. She would stay up late after everyone else was in bed and frantically write the words that brought her characters to life.

That first novel lives buried deep in her hard drive, and maybe one day it will see the light of day, but that would take a LOT of editing. About the time she couldn't figure out where that first book would end another idea persisted in her mind. The one you hold in your hands, Becca and Jared's story. Before she knew it, what started as a single novel turned into a trilogy... but wait, there's more. She now has four stories drafted and several other ideas for the characters of Hazel Hill, North Carolina.

Liz's heart longs to live in North Carolina, where she was born, and that is why she set her stories there. But, for now, she and her husband live in Northern Illinois where she homeschools their three daughters.